South of the NBA

a novel by

Sean Kelly

SOUTH OF THE NBA

Copyright © 2014 by Sean Kelly

To my wife and editor, Cathy

And to my friends Brennan Hurley
and John Tomlinson

South of the NBA

Chapter 1

A Call for Help

The caller on the other end of the line sounded far away and the connection was weak. But I recognized his voice immediately.

"Craig Bailey, you're wanted by the police!"

I couldn't believe it was him. El Negro. I hadn't seen him in ten years and he had stopped writing about eight years ago. My letters to his last known address in Argentina had come back undelivered.

"Joel!" I shouted. "How are you, brother?"

"I just got out of the big house in Buenos Aires," he began. His voice wasn't quite as I remembered it; he didn't seem lucid. El Negro sounded down and out.

"Man, I'm out of money and I'm trying to get back to the States," he said. "I was calling to see if you could help me out."

El Negro was what they called him in the small town in northern Argentina where I met him. He went there to play ball after a stellar college career in the U.S. Maraviollso! Sensacional! – A professional basketball player with skills and ability not yet seen in that part of the world. He once scored 75 points in a basketball game and broke a backboard in Bolivia in front of angry military police with rifles.

Joel had been a hero and then he went to prison. I couldn't bring myself to ask what happened. I could still see the crowd after his dunk in Bolivia. Even the guards put down their weapons to applaud his athleticism. His fans were so astonished by his leaping ability they nicknamed him the Condor. And he could soar.

When we met in Argentina I told him I was an aspiring journalist looking for a story. If I'm completely honest, I was there because I wasn't ready to let basketball slip from my life. Joel's teammate from the United States was a friend of mine and had invited me to come down while he embarked on a professional basketball career after college.

"You never know," my friend had said. "Maybe you can hook on somewhere."

He knew me so well. My career had basically ended after two years of playing JV at the University of North Carolina at Chapel Hill. I got a try-out for legendary basketball coach Dean Smith as a walk-on in 1976, but got cut after a week, despite my best efforts. I knew back then it was time to move on but I just couldn't shake the game and continued to play all the time, expending more energy in the gym than in the library.

My time on the basketball court did little to prepare me for my first job, working as a copy aid at The Washington Post. I had joined in 1981, not long after Watergate and the Pentagon Papers made the newspaper famous, drawn to the excitement of working there. But when I arrived it was clear I was way behind my peers, some of whom came to the paper equipped with journalism degrees from Harvard, Columbia and Yale.

As I struggled to navigate the Post's competitive newsroom, a letter arrived from my basketball friend and former high school teammate, Jesus Barbosa. He had been waived by the Denver Nuggets, but had hooked up with a sports agent from South America. There was a team in northern Argentina that wanted him. He would be paid about $2,000 a week, in addition to free meals and a furnished apartment in a place called San Miguel de Tucuman.

"If you want to practice your Spanish, come on down and stay with me," Barbosa said in his note. "I'd like the company. I've never even heard of Tucuman."

It sounded like an adventure and I told myself it might help me professionally as well. I knew of the "Dirty War" taking place in Argentina and had learned that several thousand Argentines had gone missing as the military dictatorship sought to pre-empt a rebellion. After speaking with the Post's foreign editor for South America, it seemed there might be a story to uncover down there. We had few correspondents in the region, she pointed out, so there was less competition in the field.

I decided to take Barbosa up on his invitation and informed my family, which predictably didn't take it well. Between my parents and three siblings there were five professionally successful doctors in the family, either PhDs or MDs, and they were constantly confused and frustrated by my choices. I purposely left out information related to the possibility of playing basketball in Argentina. But I was excited to see what it was all about.

South American basketball was a new frontier for young Americans pursuing professional careers abroad during the 1980s. Political unrest was rampant across the region and it was way behind the more developed leagues in Europe, especially Spain and

Italy, which is where most elite U.S. players were going at the time. The better players there commanded six-figure salaries.

Others, playing in neighboring countries like France and Belgium, would make as little as $500 a week with room and board. But even at that rate, a growing number of players that couldn't make the NBA felt the opportunity to play professionally was worth it.

South America boasted only one widely known player during this time – Brazil's fledgling star, Oscar Schmidt. Argentina had no internationally-known players and the country fielded no Olympic team in 1976 or in 1980.

The only American of any note playing basketball in Argentina at that time was Jackie Gilloon, a player from the University of South Carolina. He had been chosen 17th in the seventh round of the 1978 NBA draft and didn't make the team, then landed in Argentina. Gilloon played for a team in Buenos Aires, where the country's most competitive leagues were. I couldn't imagine what I'd find in San Miguel de Tucuman.

Tucuman was a small agricultural city that had been a hub of political opposition to the country's dictatorship. Military rule had been in place since 1976, when Argentina President Isabel Peron was overthrown by the junta. I had been cautioned that interviewing people about the Dirty War could be dangerous. The military was said to be aggressive and quick to arrest potential sympathizers. But at age 23, I was up for the adventure.

My father, a former major in the Marine Corps,

was pessimistic about the welcome I would receive as an American. "Just assume," he said, "that they all hate you."

"Got it," I answered as I walked out the door.

I had no contacts in Argentina except Jesus, and would be staying with him while I was there. As a native of Cuba, Jesus spoke Spanish and had some relatives in Buenos Aires. Our friendship went back to high school in Washington, D.C., where we played basketball together. Jesus was a local star and a great point guard, though only 5'11."

After high school, he accepted a scholarship to a big state university, but an opportunity to play never materialized. He left the next year and played the following three for a small college in Denver. It was there that he caught the eye of a Nugget's assistant, who gave him an opportunity to try out for the NBA.

"I lasted three days," said Barbosa, who along with many other NBA hopefuls had been handed his walking papers. "They were interested in only one player," he wrote. "It was the big-back who played with Larry Bird at Indiana State." Carl Nicks went on to play in the NBA for three years on three different teams.

Jesus wasn't ready to stop playing. The offer in Argentina appealed to him because he had heard the basketball competition in Buenos Aires was beginning to emerge onto the international scene and other players from the U.S. were seeking professional homes in cities south of the equator.

The political climate in South America was a concern; Jesus was not totally accepting his uncle's assurance that he would be safe. Nevertheless,

Argentina was the only opportunity that came his way. He figured it might be a stepping stone to Europe.

"If playing in Tucuman is anywhere close to playing in Spain, maybe I can make my way over to Barcelona and get another shot at the NBA," he wrote.

My trip from D.C. to Tucuman was a long one. A flight to Buenos Aires was followed by twelve hours on a train before I finally arrived on a sleepy afternoon. In a matter of minutes, those few travelers who had disembarked moved on and I was by myself in this strange city. Not far from me an olive-faced boy stood on the platform, greeting those of us getting off. He held a wooden shoe shine kit under his arm, wore cheap tennis shoes laced through only a few holes and had unkempt black hair. The boy, who went by the name of Goat, walked right up to me, tugged on my shirt and invited himself to accompany me while I made my way outside.

"You are a Norte Americano," he said in Spanish. "Did you come to see El Negro from the United States play basketball for Villa Lujan?"

"There's a black man from the U.S. who plays basketball here?" I asked, stopping in surprise.

"Si senor," Goat said. "He will be playing for the Los Lobos. That's the name of our club's team."

"Villa Lujan Los Lobos," he added, smiling upward.

The boy, who looked like he hadn't bathed in two weeks, told me to wait where I was and that he would return promptly. I nodded and took in the English architecture of the station. My old man, a train buff, would have recognized its 19th century builder, Andrew Handyside. It gave me a twinge of regret to think about our goodbye. At best, he thought I was wasting my time.

When Goat returned, he was holding a soccer ball instead of his shoe shine kit. Business was over, time to play, I thought. As we walked along together, Goat told me many things about El Negro, but one of the things he couldn't tell me was the basketball player's real name. I was eager to find out.

"The people from Villa Lujan said El Negro can jump higher than anyone in my country," the boy said. "He is a true condor, senor."

Goat dropped his soccer ball to his foot and popped it up into his hands.

"He can fly!"

I kept walking. So did the boy.

"The people said El Negro is on his way here," he continued. "We have been waiting for him, Norte Americano. He is coming to make us the champions of all San Miguel de Tucuman."

I asked the boy if he knew of any other players from the U.S. that had arrived, hoping to track down Jesus. I had written him to say that I was coming and would find an inexpensive place to stay until I was able to locate him. Barbosa wasn't sure of his exact address, so we agreed to find each other somehow after I arrived. Goat told me that he hadn't heard of any other players who had come to town.

Then I saw the Hotel Americana, a modest two story structure with a street cafe out in front across the park and asked the boy whether it was a good place to get a room for the night. It had been a 700 mile train trip from Buenos Aires and I needed a shower.

"Si, senor," Goat said. "I have shined many shoes that have come out from the hotel in the morning and they have never told me any bad stories."

"Fair enough."

Goat kept me company as I crossed the grassy park under the hot afternoon sun. At its center, we passed a fountain splashing freshly amidst palm trees and other subtropical plants.

Also noticeable were two military soldiers, dressed in blue fatigues and holding guns, calmly watching the park and nearby streets.

A group of American journalists I met after landing in Buenos Aires had warned me to stay away from the military presence up here. Keep a low profile and everything should be fine, they said. Just don't invite trouble and get apprehended for any reason.

Most people, at least as far as I could tell, went about their business as if the soldiers weren't there. This was reassuring and I thought I'd let my father know the situation didn't seem as crazy as he assumed. Before we said goodbye at the Hotel Americana, I made sure to ask Goat where I could find the Post Office.

I spent my first days in Tucuman taking in the sights by myself. I saw Goat around town several times. He always had a soccer ball with him and you could see the boy dribbling it wherever he went. One afternoon, when the town's mid-day siesta had ended, I saw the boy coming toward me, dribbling his ball cleverly with his feet.

"Craig Bailey," Goat said, excited. "I have just come from the athletic club Villa Lujan. I have seen El Negro."

"He is here?" I asked. "El Negro exists?

"He is the blackest man I have ever seen," Goat said. He pulled out a ripe December orange from his back pocket and began to eat it, spitting seeds out of his mouth with the same precision as a pea shooter. "He is very tall and his feet are very long, and when he jumps, he shoots into the air. No wonder he is called a condor. Then he just stays up there like the great bird, spreading his arms so long that he could touch both sides of Iguacu Falls."

Anticipatory rumors about El Negro were all over town. A black basketball player was coming from the United States to play for the Villa Lujan Los Lobos. They said he is from "Flint," but no one seemed to know where exactly that is. When I suggested it could be the city near Detroit, Michigan, that didn't register either.

Some said El Negro travelled to Tucuman from Africa, where his parents were from a tribe of black men eight feet tall. He was said to have 15 brothers and sisters and killed a lion with a spear. Up until now, I had seen no black men in town, only Argentines with varying shades of skin color from pale to dark brown. I noticed that people with darker skin tones were sometimes called Negro but it meant nothing discriminatory. Negro was just another colorful nickname popular here and throughout the country.

The only black men who ever came to San

Miguel de Tucuman, I was told, came mostly from Brazil to play soccer. But those athletes could only run. Men from the neighborhood stood unified in their belief that none of the Brazilians could fly like El Negro.

"El Negro must save Villa Lujan from the humiliation of being cowards," said an older man, seated on a park bench near the train station. "They are a group of clowns, who can run fast only when their neighbors spit at them from the bleachers as they hurry for cover after losing another game without dignity."

"I have heard him talk," Goat said. "He speaks our language and his smile is big and his teeth are very white."

"Is everything about El Negro big?" I asked.

"No," the boy answered. "His waist is not so big."

Goat then held out his hands in front of him in a way that it reminded me of a man describing a fine looking woman.

"But his legs are very long and when he walks you can see his muscles stretch each time that he takes a step," Goat said. "They are not big like the legs of Jose Ramone but El Negro's muscles look rock hard."

It would be an understatement to say that sports were very important to the citizens of Tucuman. In my short stay in town, I had already heard about Jose Ramone, Tucuman's rugby hero, and his most famous game, which was played in Hawaii. Ramone scored a late game-winning try against New Zealand after he broke through the scrum and emerged in the open field. With two men holding onto him, he charged down field for 20 meters like a workhorse moving through ankle-deep muck.

"It is a funny thing," the boy said, getting back to El Negro. Bending down to grip his calf, he continued, "His muscles here are small, like the fists of a fighter. And they are up high below the knee. They are tight and strong, but I do not know any man that I have seen who has legs like El Negro."

"I have to go now, Craig Bailey," the boy said, dribbling his soccer ball down the street. "The people at Villa Lujan say the Cubano from Miami is coming here tomorrow. He is in Buenos Aires and is on his way. They say that Cubano can dribble a basketball the way Maradona dances with a soccer ball."

"But no one has seen him play, how can they know that?" I called after him. So far, I hadn't met anyone who had seen my friend play, but the rumors of his abilities were far reaching.

Goat shrugged indifferently and as a local bus drove by, he kicked his soccer ball at it, hitting its side squarely. The ball bounced back to the boy, who secured with his feet and continued down the street as though he had received a pass from a teammate. Passengers who witnessed the move from inside the bus seemed unmoved as thick exhaust plumed upwards into the city's green-leafed orange trees.

Tucuman was a small charming town and a far cry from sprawling Buenos Aires. I would have no trouble finding the basketball player named Cubano. I couldn't wait to see him and was also eager to meet El Negro. Covering the Dirty War seemed less intriguing to me now.

Chapter 2

Manuel Fiol

"That's right," Manuel Fiol said into the telephone, sitting in a book-lined study at his small ranch near the foothills of the mountains. The primary director of the athletic club Villa Lujan smiled as he reported he had successfully signed the Americans to play for his club's basketball team, the Los Lobos.

Manuel was a native of Tucuman but the grandson of Italian immigrants. He had been educated in America and had returned to Tucuman after college to run his family's ranch and oversee investments. During his time in the States, he had seen many Americans play basketball and became a fan after watching the New York Knicks in Madison Square Garden. He knew there were some black Americans playing in Buenos Aires and had decided it was time to introduce high-caliber players to the premier league of San Miguel de Tucuman.

"El Negro is here," Manuel said. "Cubano is coming tomorrow and we play Tafi Viejo on Friday. Both of them speak Spanish fairly well, so they should have few problems, my friend."

"Do you want me to check in with the Chilean, or should I give it a little more time?" asked the voice on the other line.

"There is plenty of time for that." Manuel said, lighting a hand rolled Honduran cigar. He blew some smoke out and smelled its aroma. "Tonight I have invited El Negro to come and dine with me. I want to see for myself what the condor is like. I know he can play the game of basketball, but we need to know more about this man who can fly, no?"

Manuel hung up his phone. He called for his assistant, Sara. The older woman came quietly through his dark-stained wooden office door. She wore glasses, was neatly dressed and held two slightly bulky envelopes that she handed to Manuel.

"Good," he said, accepting them. "Equal amounts in both?"

He held them up for a better look. Manuel was impressed with himself for hiring the first basketball players from the United States to play for a team in San Miguel de Tucuman.

He had gone about it in a deliberate manner. Manuel hired a scout from Puerto Rico who was bilingual and told him to intercept some of America's post-college talent before they went to Europe. He needed to find two players who could speak Spanish.

Manuel's hope was to capture a championship, a tall order as things stood. The Villa Lujan Los Lobos needed a major overhaul. They were the laughing stock of the city and he was intent on changing things. He wanted to bring in two strong players who could teach the others better skills. The presence of the first foreign players in Tucuman would also boost attendance and be good for business.

Once he had turned things around, Manuel planned to trade his recruits to another team for more than he paid. What he offered the Americans was an opportunity to play ball, earn money doing it and maybe get another shot at the NBA. It seemed like a fair deal.

El Negro was a catch. He was the only player

with NBA-level skills, talent and size that his scout from Puerto Rico could find who could speak the language. If it hadn't been for the Hispanic girl who had come to see Jefferson's last practice, the scout may never have known the black man was bilingual.

"I've just come to tell you how sorry I am that I got you into trouble, Joel," the girl had said to him in Spanish. "I drove all the way from Phoenix. I feel terrible about the entire thing."

"It's okay," Joel responded in Spanish. He recalled his involvement in a barroom fight during his team's trip to Arizona for an exhibition game against the Suns. "I know you had nothing to do with it," he added. "Stuff like that happens to me all the time."

Manuel's scout had listened intently to their conversation. He was more interested in Joel Jefferson's working knowledge of Spanish than the content. After he watched the girl hug the tall black man goodbye, he walked over and handed Joel his business card.

"My name is Rodriguez," the scout said. "I have a client in Argentina who would be interested in your services as a professional basketball player for his team there. If you don't get picked up by the NBA, give me a call if you think you might like to play in South America."

It was the best offer Joel would get. A few months later, he found himself folded uncomfortably in the cramped front seat of a black and yellow Renault taxi as it rolled down a country road outside the city of Tucuman. He watched the sun dip below the mountains, sending dark shadows over vast fields. Night had fallen by the time he arrived at his new employer's home.

The taxi made a right turn and continued up a long driveway lined with palm trees toward a hacienda that sat on a hill. The sky was full of bright stars. Joel hadn't seen so many since his childhood summers in Alabama; he never saw a sky like that in Flint. In the distance, a cloud of faint light glowed above San Miguel de Tucuman.

Manuel walked down his steps to greet Joel as the cab stopped. His hacienda was modest in size but graced with beautiful wood pillars and buttresses that supported its terra cotta roof, with wide patios at both ends. It was two stories high and had big windows framed by black wooden shutters. Lights from the house spilled out from every first floor window and two Vizsla bird dogs came trotting out beside their master.

"Joel Jefferson," Manuel said, extending his hand to the tall black man. "Welcome to San Miguel de Tucuman." Manuel quickly appraised his new employee with admiration. He was every bit of 6'8," lissome, long, a professional athlete for certain. His scout had found him exactly what he was looking for – an NBA thoroughbred.

They shook hands. Manuel gestured toward the steps and then his front door. His dogs barked, but Joel paid them no mind. He looked with interest at the impressive house, with its colonial-era architecture. "I'm a long way from home," he thought.

"I have the best steaks prepared for us by the best chef in all of Argentina," Manuel said, directing Joel into his house. "They are thick as a man's fist and fresh from the Pampas, senor."

Manuel guided Joel into his study, which was paneled in cherry wood. He had a library of books by English and Latin writers. Everywhere Joel looked there were hunting trophies – mostly deer, but there was a lone black wolf stuffed in its entirety in one corner and a jaguar on its hind legs lurking menacingly in the other. Art and decorative lamps were intermingled with the wildlife and a huge wooden desk stood at room's center.

"Tomorrow, Joel, the Cubano arrives," Manuel said, relighting his cigar, "and then you, he and I will discuss my plans to reinvent my Los Lobos and make Villa Lujan a champion."

Joel was beginning to wonder what kind of team he was joining.

"I hope he's good for the money," he thought.

Chapter 3

Villa Lujan

El Negro entered his new gymnasium for the first time with trepidation. The rudimentary facility where the Los Lobos played their games was a far cry from the venues he was used to.

Joel had tried out for the NBA. He played for the University of Michigan in an NCAA championship game against Indiana. He had competed in front of national television audiences in sold-out arenas. Now he was in a small town in northern Argentina with a playing facility that looked like some of the run-down gyms back in Flint where he played during high school.

He paused a few seconds to gather himself. Then he passed through a four foot high iron fence onto an old maroon-colored tile playing surface. He hugged a basketball to his chest and looked around.

The gym was made of scarred concrete and its tin roof had multiple patches to prevent leaking. Its floor was dusty and slippery, but of regulation length and width.

In the stands at center court was a small section of freshly painted folding wooden seats that El Negro presumed were for VIP attendees. The rest of the seating consisted of cement bleachers that could accommodate about three thousand spectators.

On the floor there were some children, mostly boys, dribbling basketballs and soccer balls with their feet and hands. They kicked, headed and bounced balls energetically, shooting at the baskets in various

18

unorthodox ways that amused El Negro.

He could see that basketball here was way behind the times. Then he wondered when his new teammate from the States would be arriving. He could use a friend.

Suddenly, in front of El Negro, a boy spun around and flipped a soccer ball from behind his head with his feet. He caught it with two hands, dribbled once and attempted a lay-up that bounced off the rim.

"Athletic," El Negro commented to himself.

The boy retrieved his ball and dribbled it with his feet through a maze of activity around the basket. As he approached the tall black man, the boy flicked the ball with his feet smartly up into his hands. He smiled at Joel.

"Can you show us something, El Negro?" the boy asked in Spanish.

"What's your name, little guy?" Jefferson answered in the same language.

"The people from Villa Lujan call me Goat," the boy answered. "It is the name given to me because everyone always tells me that I look like a dirty goat and need a bath."

People from the neighborhood of Villa Lujan standing behind the fence took note of the encounter. Play by the children slowed to a stop. Jefferson stood at half court, noticing a crowd had formed.

"El Negro," the boy said, "the people from Villa Lujan are waiting. They want to see you fly."

The black man bent down to lay his ball on the tiled surface and removed his navy blue sweatshirt, which sported gold lettering that spelled "Wolverines." Underneath, his gray athletic shirt fit him snugly and his arms had the long muscles of a swimmer. He picked up his ball with one long hand.

He turned to face the basket at the far end of the court. Gripping the ball securely in his left hand, he cocked back like a baseball pitcher and launched a hard throw at the distant backboard. The basketball struck the marked rectangular box above the rim with a resounding thump and bounced twice on its return before Joel secured it with two hands.

He swung toward the near basket and in a jog, dribbled to the foul line, where he leaped high into the air. As he floated effortlessly toward the basket, he raised the ball above his head, lowered it to his waist, palmed the ball in his left hand, wind-milled it around his head and then tomahawked it through the basket. The net flicked upward from the rim. Gravity brought El Negro back to earth.

"Sensacional!" shouted Petchie, a Villa Lujan loyalist, turning to his crony, Pata, as they stood with the crowd outside the fence.

"Maravilloso!" Pata responded enthusiastically.

"In all my life, I have never seen such a thing," Petchie said. "I did not know that human beings could jump so high. I have seen some North American black men play basketball for mighty River Plate in Buenos Aires, but none of them could leap like El Negro."

"Did you notice how long his hands are?" Pata remarked, dropping his cigarette on the concrete floor to demonstrate. "He held the basketball in one hand like it was the ball of a small boy. Then, he threw it like it was a shot fired from a soldier's gun. If it had hit you in your head, Petchie, El Negro might have killed you."

Petchie pretended to be insulted. Then with his right hand, he softly punched the side of his face, appearing to absorb the blow with little difficulty.

"No, it would not even have knocked me out, Pata," he said. "When I was younger, I was in the ring with Rivas himself, the best of all the heavyweights in Argentina. We fought three rounds before the fight was stopped."

"You, Petchie, from Villa Lujan, put on the gloves against the great Sergio Rivas?" Pata repeated, amused. "Petchie, the Human Head, emerged victorious and returned to San Miguel de Tucuman as the heavyweight champion of Argentina."

"No," Petchie said, with a smile. "Rivas broke his hand when he hit me in the head, because that is where the doctors put the metal plate. Remember when I crashed my truck into police headquarters as I came to get you out of jail?"

At that moment, a swarthy, rotund man came walking down the concrete steps leading into the arena. Standing 5'6," he must have weighed 260 lbs. and his smile was as wide as his girth. Known as Gordo, like so many big-bellied men around town, he was the neighborhood cab driver.

Behind Gordo was a sleek-looking stranger in his early 20s. His dark hair was short and neatly groomed. His long-sleeved button-down shirt was pressed and his blue khaki pants were crisp. He carried an athletic bag over his shoulder, which he steadied with one hand as he walked down toward the basketball court.

The eyes of Villa Lujan turned in his direction.

Everyone knew this must be Jesus Barbosa, the North American who had come to San Miguel de Tucuman to team with El Negro and return their beloved Los Lobos to respectability. He was already known around the neighborhood as Cubano because his family settled in the U.S. after fleeing Cuba.

El Negro, spotting his new teammate, picked up his basketball and walked over toward the gate leading to the court. He watched as Gordo, a self-appointed bodyguard, led the way for Jesus.

Barbosa received warm smiles and a few light pats on the shoulder as he walked through the crowd. When he passed Petchie and Pata, he heard one of them murmur that Cubano could dribble a basketball better than Maradona could dance with a soccer ball.

"No one can work more magic than Maradona," he heard the other say.

As El Negro walked toward him, Cubano noted the black player's impressive thighs. His quadriceps looked huge and disproportionate to the rest of his body. He had the high calves of a sprinter. His shoulders appeared normal in width but his arms were exceptionally long, even for a man who stood 6'8."

El Negro was a dark black man, Barbosa noticed. He was darker than many basketball players he had seen over the years. His new teammate was African black, with a long, narrow face and a strong jaw that gave him a chiseled appearance. His eyes were as dark as his complexion. His nose was wide and his lips, big.

To El Negro, Cubano looked athletic but not as big as many of the players he had known. He had a slender frame and stood slightly under six feet. His skin was a light olive, like one of the many shades El Negro had seen among the people of San Miguel de Tucuman. Since his arrival, Joel had seen a wide range of complexions – from white to very brown and even Indian red – but none as black as his.

As Jesus walked onto the tiled playing surface, Manuel Fiol emerged from a narrow tunnel that ran through a section of concrete stands on the opposite side. In contrast to most in the crowd, Manuel was dressed sharply in a blue blazer and tie, gray trousers and polished shoes.

His face was alert and more businesslike than when Joel had dined with him the night before. Manuel joined the two players as the people from the neighborhood looked on from outside the fence.

"Senor Barbosa, welcome to Villa Lujan," Manuel said, offering his new player a firm handshake. "Finally, you have come to our great city to play basketball for Los Lobos."

He smiled as he turned to the black man.

"Already, Joel," he said, gesturing to the crowd, "I have heard the people of San Miguel de Tucuman speak of El Negro. They say that when the mighty black man leaps, he explodes into the sky."

He shook El Negro's hand firmly and then draped his arms around the North Americans' shoulders affectionately as they faced the concrete stands.

"This is why I have brought you here," he said. "Villa Lujan is a place for champions. My grandfather was responsible for building this arena. It is the home of my family. Do you remember the great Victor Galendez?"

Manuel adopted a boxer's stance, jabbing with his left hand, following with his right. He held his hands up to cover his ears, bobbed his head and took a shuffle step up and back.

Manuel smiled at the Americans playfully.

"He was the light heavyweight champion of Argentina and one day would have held the world title if he had not died in an automobile accident," Manuel said, dropping his hands to his side.

"I thought he died in a race car accident," said Jesus Barbosa.

Manuel turned to him. His head tilted in acknowledgement. "It is true; he was an excellent race car driver. In any case, Victor Galendez's grandfather knew my grandfather. And the light heavyweight champion of Argentina fought here in Villa Lujan."

"All around you, Jesus, the stands that you see were full and there was standing room only," Manuel said, glancing all about the concrete arena. "There were people climbing the fence to get in. Military guards waved batons and shotguns to disrupt the overflow of locos from filling the arena, singing and yelling. But there was no use trying to stop them. The people of San Miguel de Tucuman wanted to see their country's champion, Victor Galendez, fight here in Villa Lujan."

"It was a happy time for my people, for our neighborhood; even the television cameras came from Buenos Aires to film this great fight." Manuel took a breath. "I want to bring such moments back to Villa Lujan. I want to see our neighborhood come alive and cheer for their basketball team and you two will make the Los Lobos the envy of every basketball club from here to Cordoba."

Manuel handed each an envelope. It was their first payment as his new employees.

"We play Tafi Viejo in two days, my friends," Manuel said. "Be certain to remember the history and tradition Villa Lujan has enjoyed over the years. It is time that we bring this happiness back to my club, back to my neighborhood and back to my people."

Manuel paused. As he did, a weathered basketball rolled swiftly between the three men. It bounced off of El Negro's leg and ricocheted to the boy, Goat. He scooped it up with two hands the way a soccer goalie would secure a kicked ball on goal.

"El Negro," Goat said, looking up at the tall black man. "Come and fly some more, we are waiting."

Joel responded with an infectious smile. Jesus, however, remained impassive, his dark eyes watching the exchange between the boy and Joel and then glancing around the arena. The Argentine noticed how observant, yet guarded, Jesus had been during their brief encounter. If he was put off by the humble facility, he didn't show it, Manuel thought.

He turned to the boy "You look like you have been rolling around with the pigs. It is time for you to go home to take a bath," he said. "And cleaning the tub after you will be a job for a bulldozer."

Chapter 4

Sopa de Chancho and the Giant

After the two players had exited Villa Lujan's modest arena, the people of the neighborhood began to chatter with proprietary pride about their new American stars. Stories about the athletic prowess of El Negro and Cubano spread rapidly. Hopes were high that Los Lobos might finally find glory and their old gym would become the home of champions.

"With El Negro and Cubano," a man said, standing at the iron fence in front of the VIP section, "we will be undefeated."

"I have seen El Negro fly with my own eyes," another said.

"What will the other teams do when El Negro soars in from the rafters?" asked a third.

Joel enjoyed the gossip even though he saw the ridiculous side to it. He had never been called a condor before. He could jump, but no one had told him he could fly. "These people down here are wild," he thought.

Neither American knew what to expect in Tucuman as far as basketball was concerned. But the physical condition of Villa Lujan and its cast of characters were a bit more familiar to Jesus. Growing up in Cuba, he had seen similar gyms in San Juan and Havana and he knew what small-time operations they could be. Barbosa was quickly forming the opinion that his playing days in Tucuman would be short-lived, hopefully just a brief stop on his way to better things.

For the present, he acknowledged, his options as a professional player were limited. Jesus had a blemish on his basketball resume that had so far deterred serious interest from the NBA. He left a Division I program after his freshman year for lack of playing time, seeking a better situation elsewhere. He found a program that appreciated his abilities near Denver, but it was at a small school that played against lower-level competition.

As a result, his college playing days had been spent in tiny Division III gyms across the Rocky Mountains, obscured from most NBA scouts. Though he had dazzled spectators with his skills, he hadn't had the exposure to help his professional prospects after leaving school.

"You have a lot to your game," a Nugget assistant had told Barbosa. "But you've been playing against students planning to be doctors, lawyers and businessmen, not Division I athletes. Your skills look terrific, but are they transferrable from Division III to the NBA?"

Jesus knew he was right. During his tryout, no one looked his way. He decided he was going to have to play his way up the professional ladder elsewhere to get another chance at the NBA. For now, teaming up with the Villa Lujan Los Lobos to play basketball for Manuel seemed as good a place as any to start.

"At least I'm being paid to play," Barbosa said to himself.

Jesus and Joel followed Gordo to his cab and they began the drive to a café where they were scheduled to meet with some other "associates" of Villa Lujan. Gordo took his role as town ambassador seriously though he understood no English, "Si senor," was his usual reply, accompanied by a wide smile, when the Americans tried to address him in that language.

They soon realized Gordo was much more interested in entertaining them with stories than listening. "I will tell you something," Gordo said, glancing at his passengers, "we have not had this much excitement at Villa Lujan in two years."

"That's because they haven't won a game in two years," Barbosa said quietly to Jefferson in English.

"I know, man," Joel said. "That's hard to do."

Gordo, who listened but understood nothing, drove on with a placid expression. He beamed as the conversation switched back to Spanish.

"So what happened two years ago?" Barbosa asked Gordo. "Was it when Victor Galendez fought at Villa Lujan?"

"No senor," the cab driver said. "It was when Sopa de Chancho played basketball against the giant, Gordo of Mitre. People from all over the province came to Villa Lujan to see the game."

"Pig soup against a giant?" Barbosa asked, bemused.

"They like their nicknames down here," Joel agreed in English. "But Sopa de Chancho is a new one."

"Sopa de Chancho," Barbosa said, looking into the review mirror at Gordo. "Was he any good?"

"Si senor," said the cab driver. "He was a good player, but the giant from Mitre was too much for him. He and Sopa went at it until finally the game came to an abrupt end and it was called in favor of

Mitre."

"What was so special about the game? Barbosa asked. "Villa Lujan was still the worst team around, right?" Gordo's jowls quivered as he turned the wheel quickly, guiding the cab through traffic.

Joel, crammed in the front with his knees level with the dashboard, noticed the cabbie had become fidgety. Barbosa had hit a sensitive nerve. The Americans would soon understand the fans from Villa Lujan took hometown loyalty to a new level. If an excuse could be made to soften the harsh realities of defeat, they were certain to find it.

"The referee should not have called the game," Gordo began earnestly. "We were starting to come on. Mitre was up by only 28 points, and the Los Lobos were scoring. Sopa de Chancho was shooting from half court, making baskets."

The cabbie took a breath.

"The giant may have had his way, but only Sopa de Chancho could shoot the basketball from half court."

Joel glanced surreptitiously over his shoulder toward Jesus, who smiled slightly in reply, amused at the idea of placing such importance on half-court shooting. If the cab driver was an accurate barometer, the people of Villa Lujan knew very little about the game.

"How big is the giant?" Joel asked.

"The giant, senor," Gordo said expressively, "is as big as a building. He is taller than you, El Negro, but much heavier. He looks like he came from the dinosaurs, emerging from the Andes."

Gordo glanced in the rearview at Barbosa who

was listening attentively, though with a grin. Joel was all ears.

"They call the giant of Mitre, Gordo, too, and he is massive in every part of his body," the cabbie continued. "Even his head is very large. There is not a gaucho hat in all of Patagonia big enough for him to wear. He has arms that are thick like big tree branches, with powerful legs. His hands are the size of American baseball gloves."

"The giant's belly is big too, but strong," Gordo explained. "He is known for letting boxers from Mitre Athletic Club train on it. Big and small, fighters throw their combinations to his stomach like it is a heavy bag. Gordo considers this practice to be part of his exercise routine, standing in the ring against the ropes and letting boxers punch away at his mid-section."

"Sometimes the giant sings while this is going on," the cabbie said.

The taxi made a sudden move, neatly avoiding a motor scooter and another cab that had stopped after a near-collision. Gordo was unfazed. He kept driving as though the near-miss was a common occurrence.

The police chief of San Miguel de Tucuman had bestowed upon the giant of Mitre the honorary position of sergeant in the department, the cabbie told them. The chief was married to the giant's older sister and thought it was best to have his massive brother-in-law as an ally.

It worked out pretty well. If trouble broke out at a soccer game, the giant would come marching into a crowd with his arms swinging, his big fists like sledge hammers. Men who chose to stand their ground against the giant didn't stay on their feet very long.

"He once fought an entire rugby team from Germany," the cabbie said. And the outcome was never really in question."

"What do you mean?" Barbosa asked. "He took on all of them?"

"Si senor!"

"Que pasa?" Joel said intrigued.

"The Germans played against Jose Ramone and his Caballos teammates," the cabbie said. "Ramone scored six tries against them. It wasn't much of a match. But it was not the rugby thrashing the Germans remember, senors. It was their first-hand experience with the fury of a volcano."

After the rugby match, when tradition calls for teams to celebrate their combat on the field, beer and food were consumed in great quantities and songs were sung in both languages. But as dusk fell, the Germans, fueled by alcohol, became belligerent. They first insulted Argentina's rugby, then its food and beer.

Tempers flared and a large beer bottle was launched across the room, striking a rectangular mirror overlooking the service bar. Glass came splashing down in waterfall fashion. The wait staff took cover as a full-fledged rumble ensued.

Big, strong men threw haymakers at each other and bodies flew over chairs and tables. The teammates of Jose Ramone may have won the rugby match, but the Germans from Trier were winning the fight.

Suddenly, Sergeant Gordo of Mitre arrived, ducking in through the door. As the massive man straightened up, the establishment went quiet. One player, who was being held in a headlock, dropped to the floor with a thud as his opponent let go. The Goliath faced the entire rugby team from Trier.

Incensed at the Germans' lack of respect, the giant let out a bellow, raised his arms like a grizzly bear and charged. The first two men he encountered got their heads banged together and he surged past them as they sank to the floor. Then Gordo picked up a long wooden table and began to swing it back and forth at a group of burly men who played in the German scrum. They huddled together against a back wall. A chair came smashing down across the giant's back and splintered into pieces.

"Gordo didn't even feel it," the cabbie said.

The Germans quickly came to their senses and wanted no more of Sergeant Gordo of Mitre. A white tablecloth was tossed into the center of the room as though it were a towel being thrown into the ring to end a fight. Gordo immediately accepted the gesture with dignity and the brawl was over.

"Damn," Joel said in English, as the cabbie paused. "I know some big, bad boys, but he sounds like he's bigger and badder than any of them."

"But Sopa de Chancho was also a big man" the cabbie said, resuming his story about the memorable game.

Though far from the human mountain that was Gordo of Mitre, Sopa de Chancho was tall, standing six feet four, with a girth that was even more remarkable.

"He looked like a walrus," the cabbie said.

Also, unlike the giant of Mitre, who was known

for a testy temperament, Sopa de Chancho was mellow, mild in demeanor. His smile was dolphin-like, perpetually cheerful. If you tried to get him angry he would only become sympathetic to your cause. Wherever Sopa de Chancho went, he made people happy. He had one major weakness, however. Sopa de Chancho's mind was almost always concerned with food.

"He ate many meals throughout the day," Gordo said, and his tastes were indiscriminate. "Beef, pork, rabbit, chicken, goat, he liked them all and there was no one in all of San Miguel de Tucuman who was more pleasant to enjoy a meal with."

"He could eat more than any man in my country," the cabbie said. "Everyone at Market de Tucuman wants to have Sopa de Chancho try some of their food. If he says he likes it, the people know that such an endorsement is good for business."

Despite his weight, Sopa was surprisingly light on his feet and had good hands. Nevertheless, the basketball game between Villa Lujan and Mitre was a mismatch from the start.

The giant ran like a determined steer up and down the court, catching the ball from his teammates and putting it into the basket with two hands, the way a mason would place a large stone on a high wall. His team quickly took the lead and extended it as the game went on.

There seemed to be nothing the Los Lobos could do and Sopa de Chancho began to have trouble keeping up. He stopped running and hunkered down at one end of the court, playing either offense or defense, whichever was needed.

"Still you had to keep an eye on him," Gordo said. "Sopa de Chancho was a tricky player."

Sometimes he would stop behind half court and launch a shot toward the basket. The ball would sail through the air without backspin, like a knuckleball toward the plate. But his aim was true. There would be an unmistakable thud as the basketball banked hard off the glass and dropped through the hoop.

During the second half, the giant grabbed a rebound and passed it out to a teammate. As he ran down court and positioned himself low, Gordo slammed into Sopa de Chancho and the fat man gave way, falling back a few steps before gathering himself, his face flushing slightly. Sopa threw his big belly at the giant in return, knocking him back a step.

At first neither man took offense. Then Gordo, sealing Sopa de Chancho with his back, turned and held up his hand for the ball to be thrown to him. As he did, he felt something warm run down his calf, soaking his sock and seeping into his shoe. Warmth spattered his other calf. He looked around to investigate.

For an instant, Gordo of Mitre stood astonished as he saw and then felt more spillage from Sopa de Chancho's mouth. Angry, the giant raised a clenched fist high above his head, ready to bring it down upon Sopa de Chancho.

But before the blow could be delivered, the unofficial food critic of Market de Tucuman sank to his knees. A full tsunami erupted, spewing from his mouth as though it was flowing from a fire hose. Chunks of cow sausage, chicken, beans of various colors, tomatoes and even some remains of pigs' feet were discernible in a growing pool on the tiled floor of Villa Lujan.

Gordo backed up a few paces and his look of anger turned into disgust and then became concern. The people in the arena grew silent then gasped as Sopa de Chancho fell into the puddle of vomit face first and pitched to his back like a beached whale. His eyes rolled to the back of his head and in the middle of the second half, with his team down 28 points, the man who loved food more than anything in the world died.

People ran onto the court to offer help, but they were too late. An official waved his arms, signaling the contest was over and Mitre had won.

"It was unfair for the referees to award the game to the giant," the cabbie said. "If Sopa de Chancho hadn't eaten too much, we could have come back and maybe won the game."

Chapter 5

A Walk in the Night

El Negro was on the move. The tall black man blended into the subtropical night of San Miguel de Tucuman as he made his way through the dimly lighted streets of his new neighborhood. He was still adjusting to a summer climate in December and the heat and humidity made him restless.

Geographically, he was now farther south than even the Deep South he had known back in the States. Growing up, he visited cousins in Alabama every summer to get away from the streets of Flint, where his mother worried constantly about him getting into trouble. He liked his visits but learned it was best to avoid white people down there.

The streets of Tucuman already seemed a much more pleasant place to be. So far, his arrival had been warmly welcomed. He liked that children from the neighborhood wanted to touch him and asked him to fly. And the older people sent him smiles of approval. Here he was called El Negro with no undertone of racism. He thought he would write a letter to his mother to let her know things were turning around for him.

Joel's mind wandered back to his days in Alabama, where his cousins lived and worked a small farm inland from the Gulf of Mexico. It was there Joel got the closest thing he ever had to fatherly advice from his mother's brother. Joel never knew his real father. He and his mother, a fourth grade school teacher, lived alone.

Uncle Lamar would approve of the name El Negro, Joel thought.

On the farm he could play all day in the back fields without ever seeing a white person. It was not that he noticed when white people were not around; he noticed them when they were. Trouble usually followed in one form or another.

There was one afternoon he couldn't forget. He was 12-years old and he and his cousin had been fishing. They got lucky and started home with five good-sized catfish on a string. But things changed quickly. When they rounded the bend in a quiet country road, they saw an old flatbed truck stuck in a ditch. Its owner, a white man dressed in faded blue jean overalls, had his straw hat in one hand and a tire iron in the other.

Joel, who hadn't seen a white person all day, began to feel uneasy. It's different for a black person down here, he remembered thinking. Any encounter with white folks almost always led to an uncomfortable situation. But there was no way around it. The man was waving his hat, motioning for them to come over.

"Come on, boys," the farmer said, his red face round and sweaty. "Need yer help to push me outta here."

Lester and Joel laid down their poles and set the catfish in some shade. They walked over to the farmer, glancing nervously at each other. The farmer positioned the boys behind his truck and they complied quietly.

"Do you hear 'em, Joel?" Lester whispered, nodding to four screened wooden crates on the flatbed. "Bees."

Joel nodded, listening to the faint, steady hum. The farmer, dripping with sweat, came around to the back of the truck to check on the boys.

"I'm gonna let 'er roll back a foot or two after I get her goin'" he said. "Then I'm gonna punch her on into gear and give 'er what she got. You boys push hard as you can then get outta the way."

Joel stayed quiet. Lester said "yessir."

The flatbed drifted back as the farmer shifted into gear. He gave it some gas while the boys pushed with all their might. The truck bobbed up and down, slid sideways some. Then its tires bit, allowing the farmer to drive back onto the road. Lester and Joel watched until it came to a stop. The farmer got out and put on his straw hat.

"Come on over here, boys," he said, reaching into the back of his flatbed. "Gotta a little somethin' to let you know I'm 'preciative of yer help."

Lester and Joel approached carefully and stopped when they were an arm's length from the white man. Without warning, the farmer grabbed Joel, spun him around and held a honeybee to his backside.

"Sting a little nigger boy in his ass," the farmer said, with a nasty guffaw. "And ain't you a black nigger boy."

The insult hurt as much as the sting from the insect. Joel, frightened, struggled with the man. His eyes filled up quickly. Lester darted over and grabbed his cousin's arm, pulling him free and the boys took off running. The red-faced farmer, who stood in the road laughing, shouted out after them.

"Hey, you nigger boys forgot your catfish," the

farmer bellowed. "Want me to buzz 'em over to you?"

"Excuse me," I said in English as I caught up with the tall black man. It was obvious he was lost in thought. "Are you the basketball player from the States?"

He looked over and I stopped in surprise. I recognized him immediately, had seen him play college ball on national television several times. The tall man took a step toward me for closer inspection. His smile was bright in the darkness.

"Joel Jefferson," he answered, acknowledging me as a fellow American.

"I know! They called you 'Jumpin' Joel.' I saw you play with Ricky G, Hub, Wayman and Grodie many times," I said, as we shook hands. "Name's Craig Bailey, from Washington, D.C.

"Alright then," he answered.

"It's great to meet you," I told him enthusiastically. "Those three long jumpers you hit against Bobby in Bloomington were daggers and your dunk on the Orange up in Syracuse – no one does that in the Carrier Dome."

His smile widened. Joel was amused at hearing the highlights of his college career from a stranger on the streets in northern Argentina, where nobody knew about his past. He remembered that dunk too. It was a good one – over two people, both 6'10." A game-winner written about from coast to coast.

"Go on," he laughed. "You must be a junkie."

"I've been called worse," I admitted.

He gave my hand another friendly shake. "What're you doing down here, man?"

"I've come to meet a friend of mine and I think he's playing basketball with you," I said. "Jesus Barbosa."

Joel's eyes brightened.

"Jesus!" he said. "I just met him today. I'm on my way to have dinner with him right now. We're meeting at a place called the Rimini Restaurante. Why don't you come along?"

I was tempted, but had already made other plans.

"I can't right now," I said, turning to walk along with him. I quickened my pace a little to keep up. "But I'm glad to hear Jesus has arrived. I've been looking for him for a couple of days and heard he was on his way."

"I'm looking forward to runnin' with him," Joel said.

"He's terrific," I said. "We played together in high school. He can really handle the ball. He'll get it to you anywhere you want it. He has eyes in the back of his head."

"I heard that," Jefferson said. "You sound like you play yourself?"

"I got cut from my college team, but I still play whenever I can," I said. "I've been shooting around with some older guys in the park near Lake San Miguel."

"What's keeping you from dinner with us?" he asked.

"Truth is, I've met these girls who are studying English at the university," I said. "They showed me around town today. Now they want to teach me the Tango. I can't stand them up."

"Heard that, bro," he said. "I'd skip dinner too if

I had a chance to step out with some senoritas from Argentina. Most beautiful women I have ever seen."

"I know," I said. "Very hard not to notice."

"You walk down the street and you see a girl and say to yourself, 'That's the most beautiful woman I've ever seen.' Then you turn the corner, and the first one you pass is more beautiful than the last."

"Heard that, too!" Joel said.

We stopped at the next intersection to let a car pass. A voice called out "El Negro!" but nothing more. We watched as its red tail lights retreated down the road.

"The Rimini is just ahead," I said, pointing him in the direction. "You can't miss it. Just keep straight. I've walked by it a couple of times already. Seems like a good place."

I was curious to know how Joel was managing to communicate with the locals. I had been here a few days and hadn't heard a word of English spoken by anyone. It had been a challenge.

"How's your Spanish?" I asked. "Mine's improving but still has a long way to go."

"I'm getting by," he replied. "I'm speaking it all the time now, so it's getting better. It's all I've heard since I got here."

"How did you learn?"

"My godmother, back home, Ms. Lopez," he answered. "She came from Mexico and started teaching me Spanish when I was little."

"Got you when you were young, amigo," I commented. "Best way to do it."

Not only had I heard no English spoken during my rounds of the town, I had seen no black people. El

Negro was the first. He stood larger than life in the street. Wait until he sees what Jesus can do for him on the court, I thought. They'll be a good pair.

"Buenos notches," I said. "Tell Cubano I'll catch up with him tomorrow!"

"Wait a minute," Joel said, before moving on. "How'd you know Jesus was called Cubano?"

"Everyone knows," I said. "He can dribble with his hands like Maradona can with his feet. Talk of the town."

He was amused. He had heard the comparison.

"I don't know who Maradona is, but he must be a bad mother!" Joel said.

"And you are a condor reincarnated," I said, spreading my arms a little. "This town is sports crazed, Joel. Rumors about you two are everywhere I go."

"I know," he said. "These people are wild."

We chuckled. I clapped him on his arm. We parted after agreeing to meet for lunch the next day.

I watched as he moved along, blending back into the night. As he passed under the yellow haze of the next street lamp, I saw a young woman approaching him. I had seen her walking through Tucuman a few nights ago. She was wearing the same pair of tight blue jeans, with red high heels and a tight shirt. Her skin was dusky, but lighter than Joel's. A gold tooth glinted faintly as she stopped in front of the basketball player and smiled. She got his attention immediately.

She turned her cheek for Joel to kiss. He didn't hesitate, bending down to kiss her face gently and quickly. I could see his smile. She stood close to him.

They began to talk and El Negro allowed her to brush up against him slightly. There was no doubt she had practiced this scene before but it didn't seem to matter to Joel.

Suddenly, headlights turned toward them from a side street and the couple was caught in their glare. A small pickup truck pulled up beside them. It was a working truck with a dent in its bumper. The passenger door opened and remained that way.

The woman said something to Joel and offered her face for the black man to kiss again. He complied. She hurried over to the open door and ducked into the pickup. It drove off. El Negro stood by himself for a moment, watching.

"Don't know if I'd open that can of worms," I thought.

Joel walked on.

Chapter 6

First Dinner at the Rimini

El Negro arrived at the intersection of Balcarce and Marcos Paz, where he came upon the Rimini Restaurante, his new kitchen away from home. The cost of meals for both American basketball players at this restaurant would be picked up by Villa Lujan. Breakfast, lunch and dinner were on the house.

The Rimini was Rapido Franco's place; the fast-talking proprietor took pride in serving families from the neighborhoods throughout San Miguel de Tucuman. His establishment offered inside and outside dining, with small tables lined up along a sidewalk adjacent to the main restaurant in a modest one-story red brick building. Under the night sky, white napkins and silverware glowed in the darkness under flickering candles in brass holders.

El Negro could hear music coming from inside. It was the traditional Latin sound of a single acoustic guitar accompanied by the voice of a balladeer. This was new for him. He looked with interest for the musician as he proceeded through the building's side entrance, which required him to duck underneath its short, angled doorframe.

Joel was looking forward to dinner with his new teammate, Jesus Barbosa. A unique bond had already formed between them. Their basketball situation was shaping up to be unusual, at best. And the country was in the midst of some kind of political unrest, the details about which Joel didn't really know. But there was no ignoring the presence of armed military soldiers around town.

The Rimini was packed, with patrons at every table. Waiters were bustling about, some carrying trays to and from the kitchen. The guitar player, seated at a table near the front door, stopped singing when he spotted El Negro standing across the room. Diners ceased eating; the Rimini went still.

Joel absorbed the roomful of quiet faces and eyes. There was innocence in their stares. For a brief moment, the only audible sounds came from the kitchen grill, sizzling, popping and crackling with Argentine beef. From his out-of-the-way table, Jesus Barbosa watched with amusement as the provincial crowd appraised the 6'8'' black man.

Jesus wondered what someone like Joel was doing playing basketball in this small city land-locked in northern Argentina. To his knowledge, no other Americans with Joel's size and skill had ever played for a team in San Miguel de Tucuman.

Then a small boy from the back of the room broke the silence in the restaurant. Standing on his chair, he pointed across to Joel, calling out "It's true then, what Goat has told me. He said a great condor is coming to his neighborhood, a human who can fly."

The boy's family grabbed the youngster to quiet him, but before they could sit him down he managed to add: "That is why El Negro will bring a championship to Villa Lujan."

Joel produced an embarrassed smile. Its infectiousness stole the room. Unexpectedly, patrons began to clap their hands, welcoming the tall black man. Rapido Franco walked over to shake hands with him and raised Joel's long arm like a champion boxer.

El Negro acknowledged their warmth sincerely. Dinner in the main dining room resumed.

Rapido Franco showed Joel to his seat. Jesus thought they made a comical pair as they approach his table. One was short and plump and waddled as he walked while the other was tall and svelte, with a long gait. Joel looked a little like a race horse being led by its trainer through a crowd of curious onlookers. As they passed by, people surreptitiously took a second look at the town's new celebrity.

Rapido Franco was excited to have the Americans as permanent guests at his restaurant. He planned to feed them well. After all, they had come to San Miguel de Tucuman to play basketball for the Los Lobos and bring a championship to his own Villa Lujan.

Jesus, who had been seated against the wall, stood up to shake hands with El Negro when he arrived. Rapido Franco turned and called for a waitress. Marta arrived quickly, wearing a dark gold apron over black trousers and a white shirt. Her thick glasses magnified severely crossed eyes. Although she was taller than Rapido Franco, Marta stood timidly at attention, awaiting instructions. She flashed a shy look of wonderment at the Americans. When they smiled back, she blushed and lowered her eyes.

"Marta, these are our new friends," Rapido Franco said with authority, wanting to impress his American guests. "They have come to play basketball for Villa Lujan and will be eating all of their meals here. I have arranged everything with the directors of Villa Lujan, so keep a separate account for them."

"Marta will see to it that my Rimini is your

kitchen away from home," said the short proprietor, turning to the Americans. "And then you will see for yourselves that Rapido Franco serves only the best for the best in all of San Miguel de Tucuman."

Rapido Franco turned to Marta, spoke to her quietly and excused himself. Jesus and Joel sat down for their first dinner together. Both men ordered steak, potatoes and salad. Marta took the order and returned with a large bottle of beer and a half liter of white wine, accompanied with a small spray bottle of mineral water. Then she placed a wooden basket of warm bread and butter on the table and followed with a plate of grilled sausage sliced for easy piercing with a fork.

"That was quite an entrance, Joel," Jesus said. "Ever had a reception like that in the States?"

"Not even in college," Joel said laughing. "I didn't know what to expect when I got here. But these people down here are like little kids when it comes to basketball."

Marta returned with a glass container of regional olive oil, which she poured over a platter of fresh vegetables – red and yellow peppers, green squash, spinach leaves, sweet onions and small round tomatoes – garnished with chunks of boiled ham. The salad was topped with fresh goat cheese and bacon chips diced and smoked earlier that day in the kitchen.

"I've only been in this country for a few days and every meal has been great," Joel said in English. "And the steaks! I mean the food is incredible."

"No one goes hungry in Argentina," Barbosa responded. "My uncle said even the poor eat well."

Joel poured some beer into his glass and offered to do the same for his new teammate. Jesus declined, pouring himself some wine. El Negro watched as he topped it off with a splash of mineral water from his spray bottle. Joel had never seen such a beverage back in the States. There was already a lot to get used to.

"It took me a second when I first saw you at the gym," Jesus said in English. "Then I recognized you as soon as you jumped. I saw your dunk against the Orange up in the Carrier Dome. The networks kept showing the replay of you going up in slow motion, it was unbelievable."

"Over two big dudes, too," Jesus added.

Now that he had seen Joel in action, Jesus was convinced he was something special. The ease with which he elevated was a surprise even for Barbosa, who had seen many leapers over his years. He had even caught some of the legends playing in Harlem during the 1960s, while he was visiting cousins in New York.

Jesus would never forget Earl "The Goat" Manigault, who at only 6'1," could dunk the ball with one hand, catch it with the other and dunk it again, all in the same jump. And 6'5" Herman the "Helicopter" rose so high he could snatch a quarter from the top of a backboard. He saw him do it alongside a neighborhood kid named Bernard King.

He could tell Joel had that type of unique jumping ability. It delighted him and had him envisioning lofting high passes to his new teammate.

"A lot of people saw that play," Joel said. "Sometimes you take off just right. I don't know how to explain it. Then I had to throw it down."

Thick, juicy steaks spilling with sauce arrived. Fresh sides steamed next to them. Another bottle of beer landed in front of Joel.

"How'd you end up here? Barbosa asked, looking with bemusement at the abundance of food at the table. There was way too much for him to eat.

"I ran into a little trouble while I was in school," Joel said. "It was nothing really. I got caught stealing a chair from a dorm lobby and then I got nabbed taking a little icebox out of a school lab. We were just gonna use it to keep our beer cold. But it was enough to keep me from playing in a few games. When the NBA came around, no one wanted to take a chance on me, thought I was trouble. But Coach Bobby placed a call for me to someone with the Rockets and told them they should give me a shot."

"And they gave it to you," Barbosa said.

"I had a tryout last summer," Joel continued. "Things were going good. My jumper was falling. I was getting up and down and grabbing boards. I don't think that surprised them, though. A veteran on the team had told me to count on being in the regular rotation during the season."

"You made it then?" Jesus asked, impressed.

"Not exactly," Joel answered. "During the exhibition season, we played a game against the Suns. We were staying at this hotel on the outskirts of town. The night before we played I had some time to kill, so I went out to eat by myself. There was a low key place close by with a jukebox playing. I went in and sat in the back of the room at a table near some pinball machines."

Jesus brought a forkful to his mouth. Joel had gotten a much better look by the NBA than he had.

"The place began to fill up and some of the girls that were coming in were nice looking. Everyone was partying, but nothing close to out of control. I was minding my own business, just eating and taking it in when this blonde in a tank top and blue jeans walked over to my table and said hello. She said she was part Mexican, but I don't know."

"When she spoke some Spanish to me, I surprised her when I answered her in Spanish," Joel said. "We talked for a couple of minutes then she asked me if I wanted a bump. I said sure," he continued.

"We went out back and she pulled out a spoon and we did a couple of sniffs. That was it. No big deal. We went back in. I ordered another beer. We were just listening to the jukebox. I mean, I wasn't even partying hard. I had to get back to the hotel before rookie curfew."

Jesus listened thoughtfully, but was incredulous that Joel would snort some coke the night before a game.

"That's when this big white dude, wearing a Harley Davidson shirt, walked over. He looked like he belonged to a motorcycle gang, all dressed in black with a bunch of tattoos. He got in my face and said he didn't appreciate a nigger talking to his woman. He pulled on the girl to come away with him. She resisted and told him to leave her alone."

"He grabbed her again and she told him he was hurting her. When I stood up, the big dude grabbed me and we went over a table. He was too strong to wrestle, so I popped up to my feet and began swinging. We hit each other a couple of times before he threw me into the pinball machines."

Joel poured some more beer into his glass.

"The big white guy dove on top of me and started punching away. But I managed to get one of my feet underneath of him," Joel said.

He stopped for a second. He looked at Barbosa. El Negro's expression grew more modest.

"I have pretty strong legs," he said softly, "so I kicked him upward with everything I had and he flew off me and landed on top of another table."

Barbosa was intrigued.

"By the time I bounced up, I could hear police sirens," Joel said. "They grew louder. When he got to his feet, he looked surprised. I don't think he had been sent through the air like that before."

"Did you get out of there?" Jesus asked.

"I told him the police were coming and the next move was his," Joel said. "Instead of calling it quits, he threw a haymaker and we went at it again. But I landed a hard left to his cheek and he went down. That's all that the police saw. They arrested this nigger and let the white boy go. The Rockets found out about it and gave me my walking papers."

"Damn, too bad," Barbosa said sincerely.

"That's when this man came up to me and gave me his card," Joel said. "He had heard me speak Spanish with the Mexican girl. He wanted to know if I'd be interested in coming here to play. I had nothing else going on so I said yes. Manuel phoned and here I am."

"What about you?" Joel asked. He held an empty

bottle of beer for Marta to see. She fetched another quickly.

"I tried out with the Nuggets in a cattle call for undrafted players," Barbosa said. "I didn't make it through the first set of cuts. But my game must have attracted some interest. Some man who said he was a sports agent representing teams from South America introduced himself to me in Spanish. When I replied in Spanish, he gave me his card. He said he had a team in Argentina that would be interested in having me play for them."

"Rodriguez?" Joel asked.

"That's the guy," Barbosa said. "Not many scouts from South America around. But I want another crack at the NBA and to get there I knew had to play somewhere professionally. Even though I didn't know anybody who had played in South America, my uncle in Buenos Aires thought it could be a great opportunity.

"'It will be like going home,'" he told me. "But you know what, Joel? My uncle knows about as much basketball as Gordo, the cab driver. He knows nothing, he's an economist."

Joel raised his glass. He toasted Barbosa and took a long swig. Jesus joined with a sip of wine.

"I lived in Havana when I was really young," Barbosa recalled. "But every summer I would visit an uncle in Miami. He was the county supervisor for Riverside Beach Recreation Area. I learned to play basketball there. But I couldn't speak English then, so I played with my Cuban friends until we moved to Washington. We left Cuba for good because my dad didn't like what Castro was doing and got run off the island. It was either that or land in jail."

"That's crazy," El Negro said, listening sympathetically.

"During high school, I transferred around, trying to find a school that was a good basketball fit," Barbosa said. "I just wanted to play ball. One coach didn't want me around because my hair was too long. He thought I was a hippie, doing drugs. I couldn't stand that coach. I had a chance to get back at him and lose a game that year."

"Lose a game on purpose?" Joel asked, with incredulity.

"I thought about it," Barbosa said. "We were down one and I was fouled shooting with no time left on the clock. When I got ready for the first free throw, I looked at my coach and his expression was worried. He didn't trust me. He was pathetic.

"So did you brick 'em? El Negro asked, with a grin.

"I sank them both and we won by one," Jesus said. "I'd be lying if I told you I didn't think about missing them, but the game, my teammates, you know, I couldn't do it . . ."

"I know," Joel said. "Got to do the right thing or the magic's gone."

"During those years, my playground coach saved me," Barbosa said. "He took me under his wing and told me if I ever had a bad experience like that to remember I love the game more than I hate the coach. He kept telling me that if I put in the work, I might be able to play in the NBA. I don't know if I can, but I want to find out."

"I do too," Joel said. "I'm not planning on being

south of the NBA for too long myself. Definitely want another shot. We've got to make this thing work. Play great ball, not just good ball. It's time to make the Los Lobos and Villa Lujan champions."

Barbosa chuckled.

"We'll see what kind of personnel we have tomorrow," he said. "We won't have Sopa de Chancho, though."

"I'd like to have met the big fellow," Joel said. "With food this good, I can understand why someone could become 'adicto.'"

Barbosa eyed Joel as he worked steadily through his dinner.

"I've had some other run-ins with the law," Joel confessed, as a way to continue their conversation. "It was stupid stuff. Always is."

El Negro told a story about being arrested as a young teenager. He was caught with a handgun. It wasn't his. It didn't matter. He had followed some older boys around and agreed to be their lookout when they went into a convenience store to "conduct some business." Police had it staked out and rushed in from all directions. There was a chaotic scene, with kids fleeing left and right. When it ended, Joel was by himself, holding a gun that had been thrust in his hand in the confusion.

"I saw a bunch of police aim their weapons at me," Joel said. "It was wild. One of them yelled, 'Drop the gun and get down on the ground.'"

"What'd you do?" Jesus asked, with surprise.

"When the police tell you to get down on the ground, get down on the ground,'" Joel said matter-of-factly. "You learn that first thing back home."

"That must have scared the hell out of you," Jesus said.

"I didn't even know the gun was in my hand until the police arrested me," Joel answered. I was just a kid, not sure what was going down."

"After that, my mom decided it was time for me to have a mentor," Joel explained. "But even though she tried, I just wasn't down with that either. She made me go on rounds with this city detective. I saw some pretty gruesome stuff, and after one night, I just couldn't do it anymore."

"It was bitter cold out and parts of the river were frozen," Joel recalled. "You could see chunks of ice floating by. The hawk was coming off the water hard. I mean, it came up your pants, chilled your legs and then froze the rest of you. No one was out. It was too cold."

Barbosa listened impassively.

"When we drove around this corner, the detective stopped his car and put it into park," Joel said, eating less heartily now. "There was this body on top of a manhole cover. He wasn't moving."

"Better go check this out, Joel," the detective said.

"We got out of his car and went up to the man. He had a half bottle of cheap wine in his hand. He eyes were open, but his face was stuck to the sewer grate, frozen there from his vomit. He died like that, frozen stiff, unable to move. Kind of did a number on me."

"What did the detective do?"

"He gave me a little speech," Joel said, remembering his words to himself. "This is what will happen to you if you don't change your ways. Stay out of trouble, stay in school; drugs and alcohol kill, Joel. Just look at this poor guy."

Joel paused and Jesus eyed him thoughtfully, wondering if his teammate was going to be able to stay out of trouble in Argentina.

"Amigos, did you get enough to eat?" Rapido Franco asked, stopping by during his rounds with customers. The Americans stood up, satisfied.

"I had the chef prepare your steaks personally," Rapido Franco said. "The best beef you have ever had, no?"

"Delicioso," Jesus said.

Joel finished the remainder of his beer and set the empty glass on the table.

"And you, El Negro," Rapido added. "Our cerveza is not the American's Budweiser, but it is drinkable, no?"

"Good and cold," Joel said.

"Then maybe you are now ready for some dancing," Rapido Franco said.

"That reminds me, Jesus," Joel said, turning to Barbosa. "I met your buddy Craig Bailey on my way over here. He said he'd meet us for lunch tomorrow."

"Great!" Jesus said, smiling at the news. "He is here."

Rapido Franco warmly embraced the basketball players as they exited the Rimini. They stood for a moment at the corner of Balcarce y Marcos Paz. Even though it was after midnight, Tucuman was still lively. Cars were passing by. There was a glow of light down the street, coming from Town Center.

"What are you going to do now?" Joel asked.

"Think I'll go back to my apartment to get some sleep," Jesus answered. "Still a little jet lagged."

"How 'bout you?"

"Don't know," Joel said. "Think I'll walk around some before I head back to the pad."

Chapter 7

The Los Lobos

Gordo drove his cab up to entrance of the Villa Lujan athletic club and parked. Joel and Jesus climbed out, walked through an underpass and down a section of concrete stairs to the gymnasium. It was still early and the arena was relatively quiet. The empty bleachers encircling the floor looked even grimmer than the day before, when they were obscured by people milling about.

On the court, an assemblage of Los Lobos basketball players were shooting around, challenging each other with a move here or there. One player sent a ball toward the basket with his foot. An older man in street clothes stood by, glumly watching the players. He was balding on top with tufts of white hair sticking out on the sides.

"He looks like a clown," Joel said.

"I think that's our coach," Barbosa answered. "What else would he be doing here?"

The Americans continued to watch the play for a minute then walked onto the court. Their new teammates abruptly ceased what they were doing and turned to face the newcomers. Joel and Jesus stood together in the sudden silence and appraised their new squad, while the Argentines from Villa Lujan looked back curiously. The old man with white hair, a bit heavy set, limped over on a bad knee and held out his hand to the American basketball players.

"El Negro and Cubano," he said, "I am Coach Fernando Humberto Costillo, but my friends call me

Tortuga Viejo (old turtle). These are your new teammates and you'll see they are very worthy basketball players. As for me, I am old and have hair growing in my ears. But my spirit is still young. We begin our quest for a championship today with your arrival, Amigos. Welcome to Villa Lujan."

As the Americans shook hands with everyone, they commented in English to each other under their breath about their new teammates and coach. Tortuga Viejo seemed affable enough. Whether or not he could coach was unclear. His players, however, were a different matter altogether. Joel and Jesus had already seen enough.

It was an eclectic group that included the player seen earlier kicking the ball at the basket. He was 5'10" and appropriately nicknamed Cabezan (fat head). Next came Flaco (skinny), who was terribly thin, about 6' and had a two-handed jump shot and Romano, who was only 5'7", had a push shot from the waist, but also seemed to possess some speed.

Tanco, a former Navy man, was stocky in stature and the elder statesman of the group. Joel smelled alcohol on his breath. Tanco looked pretty rugged, maybe an enforcer type, but had trouble dribbling without looking at the ball. L'Italiano, a descendent of Italian immigrants, was a 6'1" sinewy forward who looked fleet of foot and showed some skill with the ball, but appeared to have one major problem; he was scared of his own shadow.

Filling out the roster were Augusto and Paco Suarez, brothers who were just out there running around. Neither was any good and Tortuga Viejo whispered to the Americans that Augusto and Paco were "automatic turnovers."

"If the ball comes their way and they do not pass it to the other team, it is considered good playing by them," he said. "I tell them to throw it up at the basket if they can think of nothing else to do with it. Maybe it will go in."

"We call that a 'self-check' where I'm from," Joel said in Spanish, with a slight chuckle.

As practice began, Joel and Jesus quickly ascertained the basketball IQ of their new teammates and began to call out instructions. The Los Lobos lacked basic fundamentals, were uncertain about pick and rolls and the premise of passing and screening away from the ball was completely foreign to them. To complicate things, the Americans had to use their second language to explain the finer points of the game.

The coach was not much help. "Let's go with the basketball up and down the court," Tortuga Viejo barked. "Then we put the ball in the basket."

He was a little short on specifics but his players responded and everyone began running up and down the court, shooting and rebounding as they went.

At one point, Barbosa lofted a high pass to Joel, who floated upwards with ease. He caught the ball above the box and with two hands dropped it into the basket, parting his hands outward like wings, allowing the ball to fall through gently. The Los Lobos players had never seen anyone jump that high before and they began whispering among themselves with wonderment.

"Do you see that?" Manuel said to his large middle-aged friend. They were sitting alone in the

VIP section of the stands, watching practice from the arena's shadow. Manuel's companion was also his confidante. Jefe was well known around the province and lived on a farm outside of town, with the best wine collection in the region.

"El Negro can soar," he responded. "There is no one in all of Argentina who jumps like that."

"I told you," Manuel said. "But did you see how perfectly the Cubano placed the pass for him? Listen to me, when the Los Lobos begin the season this Friday, we will win our first game. Then the people will know, my friend, and everyone will want to come see our team play. Villa Lujan will be filled to capacity soon and a ticket at the gate will be the most sought after in town."

With warm ups over, Tortuga Viejo blew his whistle and summoned his players to midcourt. Jesus and Joel jogged over to join their new teammates. The motley crew was dressed in an assortment of colors, no practice wear, and canvas sneakers. Almost no one in the States played in canvas sneakers anymore. Even Chuck Taylors had moved over for the new and more protective leather basketball shoe.

"They look like they belong in a circus," Jesus commented under his breath.

"Okay," Coach Tortuga Viejo said. He stood in front of Joel and Jesus and then looked at the rest of his team. His focus returned to the Americans and, with his team standing behind him, he said: "Now what should we do?"

Jesus looked at Joel while the Argentines from Villa Lujan stood quietly, awaiting instruction. Joel simply gave a shrug and a raised brow. Since this was their first practice together, the Americans were uncertain about which of them should take the lead. Finally, El Negro broke the silence.

"Go ahead, Jesus," Joel said in English. "You get 'em together and I'll catch your back."

Barbosa stepped up and Tortuga Viejo snapped to attention. The rest of the Los Lobos followed, looking on attentively. Joel towered from the rear but kept a low profile, content to let Jesus take charge. Manuel and Jefe watched from their shadowy perch with some eagerness, hoping to observe some advanced basketball instruction.

"Let's just play five on five, Joel," Barbosa said in English. The Argentine players' eyes grew big. They looked confused; no one had understood a word that Jesus had said.

"Sounds good," the tall black man agreed. "Let's run and see who can play, that's the only way we're going find out."

Jesus then addressed the team in Spanish: "Let's scrimmage full court," he said. "Cinco-a-cinco."

The team was divided into two groups, but they were one short for a full court game of 10. Just then, a teenage boy, about 6'1", appeared from the gym's tunnel entrance wearing Adidas leather basketball shoes. Jimmy Rubio had thick black hair and wore a rawhide necklace with a turquoise stone. As he jogged over to the circle, it became clear he was still growing. His torso looked small compared to his long arms and legs and his feet were disproportionately large.

He couldn't have been more than 17, but Joel and Jesus were quick to see his potential. He looked like he might have some game. Tortuga Viejo put Rubio on the team with four players and the group of 10 began to scrimmage. As Tortuga Viejo hobbled toward a bench in front of the iron fence, he spotted Manuel and Jefe in the VIP seats. He gave a wave. It was returned by Manuel but Jefe made no acknowledgement.

Barbosa raced down court, dribbling the basketball with ease. El Negro ran on the wing. L'Italiano, guarding Joel, stayed with the tall black man, but at the same time kept his distance. Jesus sent a chest pass to Joel, who caught it and made a move toward the hoop. L'Italiano made no attempt to stop him. He simply retreated and even raised his arm for protection against being bumped by the bigger man.

As Joel dribbled by, he could have dunked the basketball, but saw Romano spotting up with his feet set to the left of the outside arc. El Negro threw a pass to him and the short guard, wearing knee high soccer socks, caught the basketball and launched a push shot from his waist. The ball spun backwards and cleanly found the basket for a deuce.

"We can use that against a zone, Joel," Barbosa called out in English. "Pretty nice rotation on the ball."

El Negro agreed and kept running to the other end of the court. Jesus caught up to him.

"But the guy who just ran away from you looked scared to death," Jesus said.

"We got a couple of different names for that in the 'hood," Joel responded in English. "Have to toughen that one up."

Cabezan, who had earlier showed he could

dribble a basketball with both feet, was limited with his hand skills. He could dribble only with his right. But what he lacked in fundamentals, he made up for with his aggressive, rough and tumble effort.

"If we can get him to block out and set screens, we can use him," Barbosa said. "He's built like a fullback."

"Plenty strong," Joel agreed.

Flaco, the skinny 20-year-old, played hard. He got into the thick of things whenever he could. During the course of play, the slight Argentine challenged El Negro for a rebound, but merely bounced off of the muscular black man and went sailing out of bounds into the iron fence. When he got up, he had a bruise beginning to swell on his forehead. He shook it off and scored twice with his two-handed jumper.

"If he's open in the corner like that and I'm hanging around underneath, he should shoot that," Joel said to Barbosa.

Tanco, the former Navy man, stayed around the foul line and drifted into the lane during the course of play. He was slower than the rest, bumping whoever came his way. When he caught the ball, he had one move – an unorthodox-looking hook shot off the right side of the basket. Sometimes it would hit too high off of the glass and sail to the other side of the basket without touching the rim. Sometimes it wouldn't make it high enough and clanged off the rim's bottom. But Tanco would always follow his shot, delivering an illegal bump or shove into the backs of bodies gathered underneath for the rebound.

"Five fouls when you need them," Barbosa commented.

"He can definitely bang around down in the lane and cause some trouble," Joel said. "He'll be useful if we can get him to do it the right way."

And then there was Jimmy Rubio. The Americans had dubbed him "the Kid" because he could run tirelessly and had a lot of spring in his step. He managed to leap up from behind Tanco and snatch a high rebound. The boy then spun nicely with the ball and put up what he thought was an open turnaround shot.

But Jimmy "the Kid" Rubio saw a sudden flash of black soar into the air, a long arm stretched out high, reaching. El Negro blocked the ball but instead of sending it out of bounds, the black man cupped it in his hand and secured it with his other, still floating upwards for an instant before coming back down.

Play stopped.

"Nice move," Joel said to the kid, handing the ball back to the boy. "You need to use a pump fake before you shoot – like this," he added, showing Jimmy how to do it.

"Already I like what I am seeing," Manuel said to Jefe. "I wanted to bring in some American basketball players who could speak our language so they could instruct this circus act on how to play basketball. But this is even better than I had hoped. We have a black man who can fly. People from all over the region will come to see him play."

"And the Cubano," Jefe said, pulling a cigarette out of a pack and lighting it. He took a puff and exhaled. "He is quick and shifty and can deliver the ball. With those Americans, the Los Lobos will become the team that everyone will want to beat."

Coach Tortuga Viejo made his way back onto the court, motioning for his team to join him. By now, people from around the neighborhood had gathered to watch. A group of children looked on from behind the iron fence, waiting for a chance to play on the court. Joel gave them a short, friendly wave and the little ones giggled in response.

"Okay team," Tortuga Viejo said, his face even more comical at close range. "We play Tafi Viejo on Friday. I do not know too much about them. We can figure that out later. Right now, we will plan to show them that Villa Lujan is going to be the champion of all of San Miguel de Tucuman. So, tomorrow take the day to rest, but be ready come game time, my friends. We must not let the neighborhood down."

He dismissed practice. Children scrambled quickly onto the court and headed for the Norte Americanos. Jesus and Joel were patient with their questions and their desire to touch them and look them over from up close. Joel's feet were an attraction. And a little girl fingered his skin. She looked up at El Negro and smiled.

One of the kids looked familiar, however. He was dirtier than those around him and had pushed his way to the front of the pack, holding his soccer ball securely. Joel noticed the boy and also saw he was wearing the same pants and shirt as the day before, with fresh fruit stains that resembled water colors.

"Did you fly today, El Negro?" asked the boy in the dirty clothes. "I saw you leap above the basket yesterday like you were in flight."

"I thought Manuel told you to go home and take a bath," Joel said, recognizing the boy.

Goat was impervious. He dropped his soccer ball and measured El Negro's feet with his small hands.

"I will tell you something, El Negro," Goat said, peering up from his crouched position. "For you to have your shoes shined here in Tucuman, it is going to be expensive. I will charge you less for my services than all the other chicos with their shoe shine kits along the park. I am your friend. You can trust me."

Meanwhile, Jesus walked through the iron gate and stood next to Gordo, the cab driver, who leaned against its railing a safe distance away from the activity on the court. Manuel and Jefe walked down an opposite set of concrete steps and headed in their direction.

Jefe was wider and bigger-shouldered than Manuel. His love for food and wine was apparent in the size of his girth. Barbosa could see that Jefe was attentively listening to his companion, who spoke to him with animation as they walked around the iron fence to where he was standing.

"Gordo, get moving, go wait by your taxi," Manuel said emphatically, dismissing him directly. The stout little man departed without hesitation. Jefe stood beside Manuel and they took up positions on the fence next to Jesus. Manuel called for Joel to join them, which he did from the other side, remaining on the basketball court.

"Gentlemen this is my uncle, who helped raise me when my father was called into military service," Manuel said. "Jefe was a middleweight fighter in his younger years. He grew up in this very gymnasium. This is his home. He has just now watched you play basketball for the first time and he thinks, as I do, that you will help bring a championship to Villa Lujan."

"Cubano," Jefe began, "you have the eyes of a midfielder, the speed and quickness of a striker and the feet of a well balanced fighter."

The big man put a large hand on Jesus' shoulder and gave the lithe basketball player a little shove. Barbosa bounced a step backward but never lost his balance, gathering himself instinctively on the balls of his feet.

"There, you see, Manuel," Jefe said, smiling, showing teeth that were discolored from years of smoking. "He bounces on his feet like a boxer."

"As for you, Negro," Jefe continued, holding out his hand for the black man to shake, "you defy gravity. I do not know where you learned to jump like that, but I have never seen a human leap from the ground the way you do. For you to fly the way you do your mother must have fed you bird seed when you were a baby."

Joel shook hands with him firmly.

"We have our first game Friday, the day after tomorrow, amigos," Manuel said, looking fondly at his investments. "We must show the entire city that the Los Lobos, with their new teammates," he paused and slapped Jefe on his back, "are a team that will take on all comers and challenge for the Independent League Championship."

"Manuel," Jesus interrupted, "these guys don't look like they've played very much basketball. You're asking us to turn them into champions and half of them can barely dribble without looking at the basketball. The only player out there with any talent is the kid, Jimmy."

"And you, Negro, how do you stand on the matter?" Manuel asked, looking like an executive who was listening to ideas from his corporate board.

"The little dude can shoot, and the kid has something to him, but the rest need work in some things," Joel said carefully.

"El Negro, you amaze me with your polite and friendly critique of these clowns," Manuel said. "Jefe and I know how bad they are. They didn't win a game last season. Tortuga Viejo knows about the hair in his ears and that's about all he knows. But he gets everyone here on time, runs practices for them and makes certain that everyone shows up for games. That is something. Believe me. You are not telling us anything we do not already know."

El Negro shot a glance to Barbosa, who caught it without looking back, keeping Joel in his peripheral vision. Jefe pulled another cigarette from his pack.

"That is why you are here, my friends," Manuel said after a pause. "You will bring all of this together. You will teach your pupils to play the simple game of basketball, you will make Tortuga Viejo seem like a great coach and you will make the Los Lobos the team that everyone wants to beat and Villa Lujan, my friends, will be sold out for championship play."

Manuel playfully pushed away from the iron fence the way a boxer pushes off of the ropes. He had a habit of doing this when he was in a good mood. He bobbed his head left and right and then threw a soft jab into Jefe's shoulder. With a lit cigarette in his mouth, the big man bounced off of the fence in response, held up both hands with fists clenched. Manuel threw an overhand right, which Jefe blocked.

He looked like he was going to counter with a playful punch, but Manuel dropped his hands. The pugilistic fun was over.

"I tell you, amigos," Manuel said, breathing slightly. "I use to love to box myself, but to send a punch through those forearms you would need a set of cutting torches."

My new young friends," Jefe said, after dropping his hands. "Please come join me Saturday night at my rancho for dinner. It will be my honor to show you around and we can also talk of Villa Lujan. I will get word to Gordo to pick you up."

Chapter 8

A Dirty War Story

It was early afternoon and the heat was already stifling. The Rimini kept its windows and doors open throughout the dining area to cool things down. There was no air conditioning. Two large standing fans blew from opposite locations. They helped to move the air around but did little to reduce a bothersome population of house flies, which flourished in the heat and made their way around the room freely. Most patrons seemed unbothered by them and simply brushed them away.

Joel and Jesus walked through the open glass doors into the restaurant. Inside it was quiet and dim. The Rimini kept its lights off during sunny days to offer a respite from the glare outside. It was still plenty light enough to see, even as the occasional cloud passed overhead and cast a shadow that moved about the room. The Americans were dressed for the weather as they would be in the States – in shorts, loose fitting shirts and sandals.

As their waitress, Marta, approached their table, she seemed more abashed than usual. People dining nearby looked askance at the Americans but not in the admiring way they had at dinner the night before. Jesus deduced the reason quickly: they were inappropriately dressed, even though the day was sweltering.

"It looks like we're the only people in here wearing shorts, Joel," Barbosa said in English. Then to Marta, he said in Spanish. "Do the people of

Tucuman wear short pants, Marta?"

"Men do not wear shorts here, Senor Jesus," Marta said, keeping her gaze on the table. "It is almost improper for you to do so."

Neither American was disturbed by the news. Custom or no custom, the sensible thing to wear in Tucuman's piercing heat was a pair of shorts. If anything, they were amused at the quaint custom.

"Just think of us dressed in longer pants than the ones we play basketball in," Barbosa offered, casually pointing to his summer shorts. "Our basketball gym shorts are shorter, so these can be long pants, right?"

Marta blushed and continued to avoid their eyes, though she grinned slightly, knowing he was needling her. Marta was honored to have been selected as their waitress.

A neatly dressed woman seated at a nearby table caught El Negro's eye and looked down into her plate. Across from her, seated with her back to the North Americans, was a girl of about 18 in a brightly colored blouse, white pants and flat shoes. Her glossy dark hair hung well past her shoulders. She sat upright, with an easy grace, and looked good from behind, Joel thought.

The older woman whispered something to the girl. After listening, the younger woman lowered her own eyes. She remained reserved, occasionally looking up to speak, her eyes retreating downward when she was done. Joel was certain she had been instructed not to look at him.

"Must be the shorts," he said to himself. It was a new feeling for him, and a nice change, that such a reaction was produced by inappropriate clothing and not because his skin was black. When people stared at him in Tucuman, it was because most people had never seen a black man in person before. There was no prejudice in their eyes.

Just then, a waitress approached the older woman and engaged her briefly. During their exchange, the girl turned quickly to peek at the Americans, making eye contact with Joel. She looked away as her mother's attention returned.

"It is appropriate for men to wear long pants when they are out publicly," Marta explained to Jesus gently. "But it is not so busy now and the people from the neighborhood know that you and El Negro are new here. I don't think anyone will mind. Tell me what you want for lunch when you are ready."

At that moment, a tall tan-colored man with wide, imposing shoulders, dark hair and a moustache walked through the open front doors of the Rimini. He was accompanied by a younger man, athletic-looking and fair-skinned, obviously a foreigner. As soon as the smaller man spotted El Negro, he nudged his companion in that direction.

"Craig!" Jesus exclaimed in English, as he spotted his friend. Barbosa stood up, meeting Bailey half way as he walked toward the table. "I heard you were in town, I'm glad you made it!"

"I sent a note to your address in Denver to confirm I was coming, but it came back," Bailey said, giving his friend a warm handshake and a brief hug. "Then I tried calling your parents' place in Washington, but they said you had left for New York and would go on to Argentina from there. We agreed we meet here somehow. I saw Joel walking not far from here last night."

"He told me," Jesus said, greeting Craig Bailey's Argentine companion with a smile. "Come on and have a seat with us. We're just about to order lunch."

"Who's the big man?" Joel asked in English, holding out a hand for Craig to shake.

"Hey, Joel," Bailey answered, turning to El Negro. "How's it going, man? This Che Che, but some of his friends call him Hombros (shoulders).

Craig turned to his companion and introduced him to the two Americans in halting Spanish. The Argentine accepted Joel's hand and offered his to Jesus, nodding amicably. He was a local basketball player who Craig had met playing pick-up in town. He sat next to El Negro and playfully compared his broad tan-colored hand with Joel's dark black one. Though not as long-fingered as Joel's, his hands were nonetheless impressive in size.

"Muy grande," Joel said.

Bailey explained in Spanish how he had met his big friend.

"You'll be playing basketball against him," he told the Americans. "Che Che plays for the Old Boys club on the north side of town. It's a team of mostly older players, who have been together for a while, but they can still go."

Che Che nodded and smiled at the Americans.

In English, Bailey added "I met Che Che at the park the other day and played some hoop with him and some of his friends. After we finished, I told him I was a friend of Jesus Barbosa and a writer."

"Then he told me he had heard about the Cubano coming to play for Villa Lujan and his magical ways with the basketball," Bailey said, looking at his friends.

"He looks more like a tight end," Joel responded in English, giving a friendly nudge to the Argentine with the big shoulders.

"Hombros," Joel said to him. "Muy grande."

Che Che nodded with his friendly grin.

Bailey explained that his new friend had some first-hand information about the military situation in the country and might be a good source for his free-lance project. Joel noticed the big Argentine had a facial scar about three inches long beneath his right eye. It looked fairly recent.

"Che Che asked me what I knew about the Dirty War, and I told him I didn't know too much, but I wanted to find out about it and then maybe write a story for the Post back home," Bailey said quietly in English. "Apparently Tucuman is home to an active opposition against Argentina's military dictatorship. This is where some of the disappearances have been taking place."

"Go on!" Joel said, taken aback by the news. He didn't know anything about the Dirty War and didn't want to get caught up in any trouble. He came to play ball.

Barbosa, on the other hand, had been warned. His Latin relatives had advised him not to get involved in anything political.

Che Che motioned for the conversation to switch back to Spanish so he could understand what was being said. The Americans complied.

"If the military picks up one of the locals for any reason and drives away, there is a good chance they will never be heard from again," Bailey explained. "That's what they mean by the Dirty War – secret police kidnapping innocent citizens, inflicting torture, killing them. Their relatives never knowing what's happened to them, and even though the military denies it, people keep disappearing."

"Che Che," Bailey prompted, "Tell them your story."

The mustachioed man told the Americans how, about a year ago, he was walking down Garcia Street toward his home late one night. It was a familiar route he took almost every day.

"I noticed a car following me," Che Che said. "I started walking faster because I could tell something was not right. Before I could get home, three men got out and grabbed me."

He gripped the air tightly with his strong hands.

"One of them was my size, holding a wooden club," he continued. "A second man had his hand in his pocket like he was gripping a pistol. He was pointing it at my heart. The third man, the driver, did the talking."

"Get in the back and on the floor,' the driver said, opening the door. Then the man with the club hit me across my shoulders and I stumbled against the car. When I turned around, angry, the man with his hand in his pocket pointed toward my chest again."

"Get in the car and lie down," the driver said again.

"This time the man with the club rammed the middle of my spine," Che Che said, imitating the motion with his hands. "I felt tingling up and down my back."

He kept his voice low as he told his story.

"I got into the car and did as they told me," Che Che said. "The man with his hand in his pocket stomped on my ankle when he climbed into the back with me. Then the one with the club got into the front and every once in a while, would turn around and deliver a blow to my back or my head. I just kept my nose to the floor, praying they weren't going to kill me."

"They drove for a long time, but I couldn't tell where we were going," Che Che continued. "We stopped on a desolate road and they told me to get out. I could make out the shadows of the mountains, not too far away. The man with his hand in his pocket pushed me toward an empty field. Then the club hit me near my eye." He motioned with his hand to his scar.

"I fell," he said. "Then they started to kick me and the man with the club slammed the back of my head and I blacked out. When I regained consciousness, I was face down on the ground covered in dry blood. I guess they thought they had killed me."

The Americans remained quiet.

"A farmer working his fields saw me lying there and he took me to his home, where I rested for a couple of days until I could make it back to town on my own," Che Che concluded.

"Damn!" El Negro exclaimed, his eyes wide. "Why did they go after you?"

"Don't know," Che Che shrugged. "Maybe because I work at the university."

"Did you report it to the police?" Jesus asked.

"That's the worst thing you can do," Che Che said. "No one knows whose side they're on."

"He's been telling me about a lot of crazy stuff going on down here," Bailey interjected. "My favorite is the 'Blond Angel of Death'."

"My uncle told me about that guy," Jesus said. "Despicable dude, right?"

"Worse," Bailey said. "If he thinks you're against the dictatorship, he'll drug you, fly over the ocean and dump you out, alive. You either drown or get eaten by sharks, if the impact doesn't kill you."

"El Angel Rubio de la Muerte," Che Che said. "He is ruthless. He even threw a couple of Catholic nuns into the waters off Patagonia."

There was a tense silence.

"But you guys don't have anything to worry about," Che Che assured them. "Not El Negro and Cubano. Everyone in Tucuman, the military included, want to see you play basketball. No one will think you are here to undermine the dictatorship."

"But Craig, you are a writer," Che Che said, half needling, "you need to keep your head down."

"He's a hoop player," Jesus pointed out. "Maybe you could join a team," he suggested to Bailey. Turning to Joel, he explained, "Craig had a tryout for North Carolina a few years ago. He almost made it."

"Not really," Bailey demurred. "I gave it my best shot as a walk-on, but I couldn't even bring it up against Phil Ford."

"Man, but Phil can really play," Joel said. "He's as good as Rickey G, who I played with at Michigan. Both those guys made all-American together and are in the NBA. If you were running with Phil, you must be pretty good."

"Yeah, well at that level, the limits of my basketball skills and lack of speed were pretty evident," Bailey said. "I only lasted a week before I was sent down to JV."

"But you are good enough to play with us," Che Che pointed out as he finished the last morsels on his plate.

"Why don't you run with the Old Boys?" Joel joined in.

"We could use you," Che Che added.

Bailey was flattered. Basketball still had a powerful appeal for him, even though he knew it was time to move on with other things. Given his size and abilities, he went as far as he could in college with the game. A chance to write for The Washington Post was right in front of him.

"You know, all three of my siblings are doctors," Bailey said. "But I can't handle hospitals. And my father has two PhDs and a Masters degree in electrical engineering, but I was never much of a student. They don't seem to comprehend anything I do. And who could blame them? Now I'm in Tucuman thinking about playing ball with you guys instead of digging for a story."

"Nothing's changed then," Jesus said with a smile. "Same guy I've always known."

"Nothing wrong with wanting to play ball," Joel chimed in.

"We play Independiente on Friday," Che Che added. "We could use a guard."

Chapter 9

El Negro and the Cripples

Che Che and Joel waited at the front door of the Rimini while Craig Bailey and Jesus remained at the table for a minute to catch up. They hadn't seen each other in a while and they chuckled at their rendezvous south of the equator. As they stood up to leave, Craig Bailey became serious for a moment.

"Listen, Jesus," he began, "Che Che seems like a great guy but he's also hoping I might be able to help him get a story in The Washington Post. I don't know him very well but he didn't get beaten up like that because he was just walking home. It sounds to me like he's a player in the opposition."

"Are you worried about anything happening?"

"No, but I did call Joanne in the Post's Buenos Aires office and she told me to be careful," Bailey said. "She said the military doesn't play around and told me not to ask too many questions about the opposition."

"You can disappear!" she told me.

"What are you going to do?" asked Jesus.

"I'm going to take her advice until I feel everything out," Craig Bailey replied.

"El Negro, did you get enough to eat?" Rapido Franco called from across his quiet dining room. He was busy, finishing up from lunch and prepping for dinner. "And you, Cubano? I have two 'Rapido Specials,' little sandwiches, you know, for you to take home."

Marta brought them to the Americans and Rapido

Franco gave a wave from the waiter's station as he ducked into the kitchen. El Negro and Jesus were grateful and exited the restaurant. Craig Bailey followed and told Jesus he would see him later as he left with Che Che.

"Can Craig play ball?" Joel asked, stepping out into the afternoon heat. "I mean, we could use him if he's got some game. I didn't really know what to expect when I came here. But it's a lot different than I thought it was going to be."

"Only two Americans per team," Barbosa said. "International rules. I already told Manuel that Craig was coming and asked if he could play with us. He said he didn't mind if he stayed with me, but that's all he can do. Maybe he'll play with Che Che. I'm glad he's around though, we can use the support."

"Yeah," Joel agreed, as the two climbed into their waiting taxi.

Gordo dropped Jesus off at his apartment in a two-story building next to Hotel Americana. It was in a great location, just a block from the train station and within easy walking distance to Tucuman's Town Center.

El Negro's accommodations were just a few blocks from there on a shaded side street. He lived on the top floor of a five-story red brick building situated across from an old Catholic Church. Orange trees lined his block and at the far end was an open green park, busy with afternoon activity.

"El Negro, I will come to get you tomorrow at 6 p.m.," Gordo said. "And then, Tafi Viejo will see the condor fly, no?" Joel bumped him affectionately with his shoulder and got out of the cab. He stood for a moment on the sidewalk, looking up and down the street. Despite the heat he was not eager to go inside alone.

"Hey," a voice called out. "El Negro, over here."

Joel turned toward the sound but saw nothing. He thought it came from the side entrance to his building.

"Negro," the voice said again. "Here I am. Quickly, before he comes."

Joel walked toward the side of the building and descended a few metal stairs that led to a basement door. Underneath the stairs was a small man with a black patch over one eye. He was dressed in dirty work pants and a long-sleeve shirt, rolled up to the elbows and in need of some stitching.

"What are you doing down there?" Joel asked, taken aback by the man's appearance.

"I saw you when you first moved in, Negro" said the little man. "Before you came, I saw the men bringing your bed to your apartment. It was the biggest bed that I've ever seen."

Joel was amused. He listened in silence.

"Your bed was so big, they could not get it in through the front door," the man said. "They had to hoist it up through the fifth floor balcony. I heard one of the movers say that 'if El Negro is such a big condor, than why doesn't he fly this bed up to his nest himself?'"

"'Because he is a human,' another answered. Then they had a boy named Goat climb with a rope to the top of that tree over there, the one near your balcony."

"I don't know you, senor," Joel interrupted in Spanish. "But you seem to know a lot about me.

What's your name?"

"Uno Ojo," he said.

Joel extended a long hand in the direction of the one-eyed man, who finally emerged from behind the stairs. One of his feet was encased in a crudely-made shoe with a thick wooden sole. El Negro had never seen such an odd contraption, but it appeared to help Uno Ojo stand up straight. As he walked toward Joel, he limped slightly and held his head to the side for a better view out of his good eye.

"Goat climbed the tree like a squirrel and then hung a big wooden pulley from it and sent a thick rope through, which the movers used to lift your bed up to the balcony and through the doors. It was quite a spectacle. Even La Gazetta had a news story about it."

"That bed does take up my whole room," El Negro said. "I was wondering how it got up there."

Just then, Uno Ojo grabbed Joel's arm and pulled him close. He motioned for the big black man to duck behind the stair case. El Negro complied slowly as Uno Ojo pointed across the street at a figure using two crutches to make his way down the sidewalk.

"That's Cabezan Monster," Uno Ojo said, quietly. "He calls himself king of the cripples. I try to keep out of his way because if you cross him, he will choke you. He has a fierce temper. He might not like that I'm talking to you."

El Negro peeked at the figure working his way down the sidewalk. His front legs were lifeless and swung together like a pendulum with every crutch forward. His head was bald and large and his upper torso was taut and muscular. His general demeanor was angry and aggressive. Cabezan Monster was appropriately named, he thought.

"Don't be fooled by the crutches, he's a lot more mobile than he looks," Uno Ojo said. "I have seen him walk on his hands for blocks at a time and as fast as normal people walk with their legs."

Just as he finished speaking, Cabezan Monster looked over and spotted El Negro, and then Uno Ojo. Quickly, he flung himself over to his hands, somehow also hooking his crutches on his old leather shoes. He hustled across the street on his hands. Then, unhooking his crutches, righted himsself and began to crutch toward the metal steps.

"Damn!" Joel exclaimed at the spectacle. "That's the wildest move I've ever seen," he said to Uno Ojo.

"I see you with El Negro, you one-eyed bastard," Cabezan Monster said. "Did you think that I would not see you hiding like you always do when I come by? Let me tell you something, Uno Ojo, if you do not watch yourself, I will come and pull that glass eye from behind that evil patch of yours."

Cabezan Monster made threatening move toward Uno Ojo, but the one-eyed cripple ducked behind El Negro. Cabezan Monster stopped in front of Joel and stared at him, while Uno Ojo peered at his antagonist from around Joel's back.

"I see that you have an eye sore for a new friend, El Negro," Cabezan Monster said. "No pun intended."

He pointed at Uno Ojo with one of his crutches.

"Has he asked you for money yet?" the cripple asked. "Let me tell you something, Negro. Uno Ojo has one good eye and he has one good leg. He uses neither. He is a beggar. He thinks people should have sympathy for him."

Joel was at a loss, finding himself in the middle of a dispute between two strange cripples. Cabezan Monster reversed himself to his hands again. Then while standing on one hand, swung a crutch in the other to try and hook Uno Ojo out from behind El Negro.

Joel finally got annoyed at the absurdity of his position.

"Hold up, you two," he said, grabbing hold of the swinging crutch. With his other crutch, the cripple flipped right side up quickly, poised for more action.

"Cool down, little man," Joel said. He handed the crutch back, but kept a long arm extended to keep the cripple away from Uno Ojo. "What's up with you amigos?"

"I am Cabezan Monster," the cripple said proudly. "I am the king of the cripples," he continued. "Uno Ojo does not speak with El Negro unless I give him permission. And, El Negro, if you feel the need to speak with any of the cripples in San Miguel de Tucuman you must come to me first."

Joel looked at Uno Ojo and then back to Cabezan Monster. The black man was easily a foot taller than both cripples. He struggled to think of a way out of the situation. He was afraid for the little cripple with the eye patch.

Suddenly, Cabezan Monster reversed to his hands, moving his crutches off to the side. He was now in his favorite position, ready for action. He could lunge from this stance to wrap his arms around an advesary's throat with his "grip of an anaconda," as he liked to say.

His talent for choke-holds earned him an occupation slaughtering goats for a farmer on the outskirts of town.

"Unlike Uno Ojo, I work for a living," Cabezan Monster announced, proudly. "I don't ask anyone for money."

El Negro took a step back, assessing his next move. Uno Ojo took a step back with him. Then, Cabezan Monster swiftly righted himself, grabbing his crutches as he did. He glared up at the basketball player.

"I am Cabezan Monster," he said to Joel, crutching away. "And tomorrow, I will be at Villa Lujan to see you fly, Negro."

He crutched on. Then he called back.

"Have you asked him for money yet, Uno Ojo?"

Joel watched with amazement as the cripple worked his way down the sidewalk toward Town Center.

"He is the meanest cripple in all of Tucuman, Negro," Uno Ojo said. "But he also takes care of his own."

Now that the immediate danger had past, he surprised Joel by speaking warmly about his fellow cripple. "I tell you, Negro," he said. "Cabezan Monster once crutched all the way to Senora's on the outskirts of town. He went to get Pepe, another cripple, some medicine from the healing woman. No one would give him a ride. It is a very long way. Then he crutched all the way back and gave it to Pepe. It was not an easy journey."

"The little dude must not be all bad," Joel agreed.

"I must go now, Negro," Uno Ojo said. "It is a good time to walk through the alley behind the square where the restaurants are. You can always find something to eat this time of day. But I will see you tomorrow night when we play Tafi Viejo. Do you know why their cripples don't come to see their team play against Villa Lujan? They are afraid of Cabezan Monster, I tell you."

Uno Ojo kept talking as he hobbled away on his wooden shoe. "He goes after them upon sight and likes to choke them until they cough for air. I'm telling you, Negro, when Cabezan Monster clings onto you, you would need a hydraulic machine to pry him loose."

"Hold up," Joel called out to him. The tall black man hustled over to the cripple and handed him a palo, 10,000 pesos.

"Here you go little buddy, I don't need it," Joel said to him.

"Thank you, El Negro!" Uno Ojo said. "I will be there tomorrow to see you fly."

Joel watched him head down the sidewalk, passing by the church before disappearing around a corner. He stood there for a while longer, digesting the encounter.

Finally Joel turned and walked through the front door of his apartment building, still thinking about his new acquaintances. Instead of waiting for the building's slow-moving elevator, he opted for the stairs. The five flights took less time on foot.

His apartment was much nicer than anywhere he had lived at home. It had two bedrooms, with an outside balcony that had a view of the surrounding fields and foothills, and mountains rising beyond.

One of the bedrooms was home to El Negro's new bed, which apparently had made the evening news when it was moved into his apartment. It had belonged to Sergeant Gordo of Mitre, the giant, and was the only one in town long enough to accommodate El Negro. The giant now had an even bigger bed because he had gotten married.

El Negro went over to cassette player and began to look through his music when he heard a knock at his apartment door. He stopped, wondering who could be paying him a call. He wasn't expecting anyone until tomorrow, when Gordo the cab driver was scheduled to pick him up for the game.

The knock sounded again. El Negro walked over and opened it. There, in her tight jeans and heels, was the woman he had met the night before on his way to the Rimini. Her dark hair looked even shinier in the light spilling from the apartment. She wore a white tee shirt that fit snugly and her smile displayed the gold tooth he had glimpsed before.

"Well, my American friend," she said, standing in his doorway. "We met last night."

"I remember," he said, intrigued by her visit. "It's Malviva, right?

"Your apartment is very big, Negro. And you have a balcony back there. Aren't you going to ask me in?

"Sure," Joel said, showing her in. "I just moved in a few days ago, so I'm not really settled. Kind of threw my stuff in a corner and left it there."

"I saw some men lifting your bed up a long rope, with a little boy working a pulley in that tree over there," Malviva pointed. "The little boy swung the whole contraption over to here. Then the men from downstairs came running up the stairs to get to the bed. Four of them got a hold of it and the boy from the tree swung down onto your balcony as they moved it into your apartment."

Joel was amused at how many people witnessed the preparations for his coming. "I'd like to see your bed, Negro," Malviva added, in a flirtatious tone. "Is it as comfortable to sleep in as it looked when it was hanging from the tree?"

When Joel showed her the bed, she was like a child seeing her first bicycle. She pushed past El Negro and sat down on the edge with a smile. Her perfume wafted through the air.

Malviva retreated from the room and walked around the apartment, then out on the balcony. Joel followed, discreetly looking her over. She looked good, he thought, as she headed for the door.

"Negro, I want to sleep in your bed someday" she said. She turned her cheek for him to kiss. "There is plenty of room, no?"

Chapter 10

The First Game

Dear Mama:

I've been here now for almost a week. It's pretty nice, although it is really hot. The people call me El Negro, the Black One, or sometimes just Negro. It doesn't bother me though, because it's not like being called a nigger.

I'm playing ball with this Cuban American named Jesus. He's a real good player. Our first game is tonight against some team from outside the city. Our team hasn't won a game in more than a year. So, hopefully we can win one tonight.

My apartment is nice. And I get my meals at a restaurant close by. The food is different, but they serve the biggest steaks you've ever seen. Also, when you meet a woman down here, you are supposed to kiss her on the cheek. I don't think I've kissed so many white-looking women in all my years in Michigan and definitely not down at Uncle Lamar's.

Manuel paid us our first installment in pesos. I went to the bank and changed them into dollars. Here is some for you, and I'll send along some more money next week. I am fine and staying out of trouble – just playing ball.

I miss the States some, but you would be proud of my Spanish. I'm getting by just fine. Wish me luck and I'll write to you about the game.

Love,
Joel

P.S. I met two cripples today named Uno Ojo and Cabezan Monster.

Before folding the letter, Joel carefully placed $1,200 in $100 U.S bills inside. He sealed the envelope and placed it next to his cassette player on a table in his living room. He was ready for his pregame ritual. He had already eaten a meal of pasta and chicken at the Rimini. Now it was time to dress and stretch, to listen to music and find that place inside that helps him soar.

He pulled on three pair of white tube socks, clean and fresh smelling, using his long black fingers to smooth them out until they looked as if they had been ironed. El Negro picked up his high tops and looked them over, checking the laces and making certain there were no twists in them.

He put them on, leaving them loosely laced. Then he turned to his cassette player and hit the play button. A song from "Kool and the Gang" came on, his favorite band. He found his combing fork and worked on his afro. Then he ate a banana and drank a half-bottle of room temperature water. He tightened up his high tops and took a few small jumps in them to make sure they felt good.

Barbosa also had his game-time preparations. He was partial to Thorlos, an extra-thick athletic sock manufactured in Statesville, North Carolina. They had such a cushioned sole it was hard to get a blister, even after a full day of playing ball in new shoes. He wore two pair. Jesus also liked to wear sweat bands around his wrists, nothing fancy, but they had to be effective at keeping his palms dry for handling the basketball.

After dressing, Jesus began his stretching routine until a car horn sounded from outside his apartment window. It was Gordo, with Joel upfront and Craig Bailey in the back. Jesus climbed in and off they went through evening traffic, a short distance to Villa Lujan.

Night was falling as the three Americans entered the concrete arena, passing by a lone charcoal grill barbecuing some great smelling sausages. Aromatic smoke wafted in a slight breeze as they separated at the entrance.

"I'll watch from the stands," Bailey said, as Joel and Jesus descended the concrete stairs to the tiled playing surface. "Good luck."

Bailey took in the scene as Gordo joined him in the stands. The arena was active. Not yet full, but busy with people. Some he recognized from the neighborhood and others seemed to be newcomers, curious to see the Americans play. Then he heard a bus pull up in front of Villa Lujan and thirty men of various ages marched boisterously into the arena, chanting loudly for Tafi Viejo.

Bailey and Gordo watched the Tafi Viejo fans fill up an entire section, a Spartan-like phalanx looking for a rumble. They were already in overdrive.

"This should be interesting," Bailey said to Gordo in English.

"Si senor," Gordo answered.

When the visiting team took to the court for warm ups, the crew from Tafi Viejo began to sing their neighborhood song. Bailey was impressed at how practiced they were as they cheered and held their fists high in unison; this was serious business.

The Villa Lujan crowd seemed unconcerned about their raucous rivals. Bailey noticed Manuel walking in, impervious to the gang from Tafi Viejo. He sat down calmly next to Jefe in the VIP section. Bailey figured he had seen it many times before.

"How are we fixed with the Chilean?" Manuel asked.

"He's made his connection," Jefe answered.

"You are my friend, Jefe," said Manuel, pulling a cigar from his blazer's inside pocket. Jefe lit a cigarette.

"Can't you feel the excitement tonight?" Manuel asked, inspecting his cigar briefly.

"It has not been in the air for a long time, Manuel," the big-bellied man agreed. "Look at the boys from Tafi Viejo; they want to beat the Americans."

"And there are new faces in our crowd, not just people from Villa Lujan," Manuel pointed out. "There is Ricardo, the sports reporter with La Gazetta. He should be at the Old Boys game against Cajas. They are the favored teams to win our division. Yet, the Americans are the hot ticket tonight."

"Our games will only become more popular," Jefe added.

Bailey watched with anticipation as Villa Lujan entered the gym to begin warm ups. They were not an impressive sight. The only matching item in their uniforms were their Los Lobos jerseys, white with red trim. They had no warm-up pants or jackets, not even matching gym shorts. He had heard Manuel was in the process of acquiring real uniforms, hopefully soon.

Bailey grinned as he saw that Joel wore a tee shirt over his basketball jersey bearing the words "Joliet Prison." His uncle was a guard at the facility and every Christmas, he sent Joel a shirt to remind him to stay out of trouble.

While the Villa Lujan players ran through layup drills, Tortuga Viejo limped over to the sideline and sat on the wooden bench in front of the iron fence. You could spot his comical figure from anywhere inside the arena. The old coach had no board for drawing up plays, no notes prepared from scouting reports and had only one assistant, a smaller and younger looking version of himself, who was also employed as the neighborhood dog catcher.

"Looks like our boys are on their own," Bailey thought.

There were two referees dressed in the usual black pants and white-striped shirts. One of them blew a whistle for the start of the game. The Tafi Viejo players, wearing matching yellow uniforms, gathered at their bench before tipoff. The din in the stadium grew as their fans sang louder, pumping their fists.

Jesus and Joel followed their Los Lobos teammates over for last minute instructions from Tortuga Viejo. Bailey could see that El Negro was easily the tallest player on the floor. Tafi Viejo had one player 6'5" and another who stood 6'4", he estimated, with the rest of the team about the same size as the Los Lobos players.

"Okay, my friends," Tortuga said nervously, "we have to play hard. When we shoot, we want it to go in. Everyone run as fast as you can and get the

Americans the ball. For El Negro, throw it to him high and then Negro, you send the ball home. Always let the Cubano dribble against the other team and go where he tells you to go."

"Do you have that, senor?" Tortuga Viejo asked, pulling Jesus aside. "I may have hair in my ears, but we both know that you know a lot more than me. So you, El Negro and I will work together." Jesus nodded. Turning to the others, the coach directed Cabezan, Romano and Jimmy the Kid to start the game with the Americans.

"El Negro," Tortuga Viejo said, catching him before he went to jump center. "Do you hear them singing? They are afraid to go home a loser to Villa Lujan. There is talk that Tafi Viejo has a secret plan to see that you do not soar like a condor. Do you know what I say about that?"

Joel waited patiently, as the officials and players took their positions at center court. Tortuga Viejo grabbed El Negro's arm again and whispered in his ear.

"I say the condor will take Villa Lujan to new heights," Tortuga told him. "You and Cubano must make the most of this team starting right now. Go ahead and fly!"

As the ball was tossed into the air, Joel sprang upwards effortlessly to secure the tip, sending the ball back to Jesus. In the stands, Bailey turned in surprise as a voice began to chatter incessantly from behind the Villa Lujan basket. He saw a little man about 5'4", dark skinned and stocky, who stood in the empty area by himself, calling out the whereabouts of Joel to the players of Tafi Viejo.

"El Negro is moving across the lane," the man said with some urgency. "Now, he is behind you, Jose. He's running up to the foul line."

This went on for the first few minutes of the game as the unruly crowd supporting Tafi Viejo sang on, pumping their fists in unison as their team defended against the Los Lobos. Then Bailey saw his friend take charge. Jesus dribbled the ball to his left, waved Cabezan to the other side of the court, and called for Joel in English.

"Fake out and come back, it will be up there waiting for you," Barbosa said.

Tafi Viejo defenders, in a makeshift 2-3 zone defense, showed confusion at the English communication between the Americans. The tall black man darted down the baseline, headed for the corner, and spun quickly. As he reversed back toward the basket the ball was up there, waiting for him. Barbosa had lobbed it with precision just before Joel turned.

The black man rose and put his long hands around the ball. Tortuga Viejo had been right, no one on the opposition could go up with El Negro. He threw it down, with a two handed slam that began at the height of the box and finished with everyone on the court except Barbosa in shock. Jesus had already back-pedaled, setting up on defense.

Bailey joined the roar from the hometown crowd. He was impressed, even though he had seen great leapers like David Thompson and Lloyd Free in pick-up games back home.

On the sidelines, Tortuga Viejo raised his hands in delight at the dunk and Bailey saw Manuel smile in satisfaction. He also noted the little commentator from Tafi Viejo was momentarily silenced and the Spartan-like toughs had paused in their singing.

Even though the score was just six to two, a new confidence came over the Villa Lujan team. The Americans were quickly proving to be too much for the players from Tafi Viejo. El Negro and Cubano were a perfect fit, with the agile point guard threading easily through defenders to get Joel the ball so he could score inside, virtually uncontested. They both showed they could shoot accurately from the outside too.

Their performance lifted the others, especially Romano, whose push shot from his waist swished through the basket with regularity.

"I told you we could use that," Barbosa said to Joel. "He's an open court threat."

As the game heated up, Bailey began to critique the players while Gordo listened intently. "Young Jimmy the Kid shows some speed and flair, but is undisciplined and careless with the basketball," he began. "L'Italiano runs up and down with good speed, but seems afraid to mix it up. Then there's Cabezan, who plays like he's in a rugby match."

In fact, Cabezan's aggressive play almost caused a skirmish in the second half. It happened when a guard for Tafi Viejo was dribbling down court on a full run for the basket. Cabezan, coming from the other side, did a roundabout run to head him off. But instead of positioning himself in front of the player in a defensive stance, Cabezan kept running headlong at the guard.

He rammed him as though he was stopping a

wing forward. The guard for Tafi Viejo took a tumble and Cabezan fell over him. Both men scrambled to their feet, fists clenched. The chorus of toughs howled their disapproval from the stands. For the first time, army guards in blue fatigues, some carrying shotguns, made their presence in the arena more visible. But then Tortuga Viejo limped rapidly onto the floor, grabbed Cabezan by the waist and pulled him over to the bench.

Manuel and Jefe had risen to their feet in anticipation of a fight, but sat down when the buildup was quelled. Tanco, the former navy man, went into the game in place of Cabezan. Tortuga Viejo leaned down and spoke to the former rugby player on the bench, patting him on the back. Play resumed without incident, partially because the Tafi Viejo players had become deflated. By this time Villa Lujan led 67 to 35.

With two minutes left in the game, El Negro had 32 points, a bunch of rebounds and blocks while Jesus had scored 25 points, with a series of cat-like steals. He also had 14 assists, according to Bailey, who had kept an accurate count even though assists weren't officially recorded at the scorer's table. As the game came to a close, the concrete stadium started to empty of Tafi Viejo fans and as it did, the arena became more sociable.

Then with seconds to go, one final aerial feat by El Negro diverted everyone's attention back to the court. A Tafi Viejo player attempted a desperate elbow jump shot, lofted high into the air. El Negro leaped up to get it, swatting the ball away at an impossible altitude. Bailey watched the black forward sail upwards quickly, smoothly. It was magnificent, and just when he thought that El Negro had reached his highest point, he floated upwards a little more, still.

"The dude can really raise!" Barbosa exclaimed in English, forgetting his teammates couldn't understand a word.

As Joel landed and the ball bounced out of bounds, the referee blew his whistle. Everyone at Villa Lujan, including the remaining Tafi Viejo fans, applauded his athletic feat. The black man responded with his infectious smile and Villa Lujan had won its first basketball contest in more than a year.

The crowd spilled onto the court after the game, talking and laughing excitedly and surrounding the two Americans.

"Jesus, I would like to see you sometime," said a young brunette, with wide, dark eyes. She had made her way through a small group around Barbosa. Hearing her soft voice, he turned in surprise. She tilted her face and he kissed her cheek.

"My name is Esperanza."

"Jesus," he answered, after turning away for a moment to congratulate a player from Tafi Viejo. Then he got caught up in a mix of players and fans, exchanging post-game niceties. When he finally looked again for the woman who had spoken to him, she was gone.

Barbosa then ran through the gym tunnel with the rest of the team. Tortuga Viejo followed, head bobbing a bit with his gait. Joel was the last to duck under and jog into the tunnel's shadow. From an upper exit ramp, Esperanza watched them disappear.

As the players cleared the floor, Manuel turned to Jefe.

"Will you go by the Chilean's?" he asked.

"He said this was a small wager," Jefe remarked. "I think he covered it himself. But I will talk to him. He told me that it would be possible to go through him for all the games. That would make it easier for us."

"Good, we won $6,000 American dollars tonight, in addition to the best gate we've ever had," Manuel said. "When did you say the Americans are coming to your hacienda for dinner?"

"Tomorrow night."

"Okay," Manuel said. "Feed them well, Jefe. They are something special together."

"Do you see how well we play when we play with big hearts?" Tortuga Viejo asked his team before he let them go. They had gathered under the concrete rafters near a wooden boxing ring, with one worn heavy bag and a semi-deflated speed bag hanging nearby.

"To our new teammates, Joel and Jesus," he said, with youthful exuberance. "To our first victory in a year, and to our goal of winning a championship. Let us keep up our hard work. We play Tucuman BB on Tuesday, so get some rest over the weekend and come ready to practice on Monday."

Chapter 11

Late Night Rendezvous

Villa Lujan was a happy place after their basketball team's decisive win. Excited spectators streamed out of the arena with Joel and Jesus walking among them, escorted proudly by their driver, Gordo. The players were showered with congratulatory comments and pats on the back. More than ever, they were the talk of the town.

"Cubano is handsome, no?" Jesus heard a female voice say through the crowd.

"And El Negro is so strong," reached Joel's ears. When he turned at the remark, he found a group of girls standing together, giggling.

Pata and Petchie, both smoking cigarettes, were waiting for the Americans at Gordo's car. Petchie greeted them deferentially, while Pata held open the front door for El Negro, then the back door for Cubano. Gordo made his way around to the driver's side and got in.

"Do you see, Negro?" Petchie said to him through his window. "Villa Lujan will soon be on top of the division." He looked at Jesus. "And Cubano, there is no one in my country who can do the things you can do with a basketball. Maradona himself would appreciate your magic."

"We will be los campeones, mis amigos," Pata remarked. As he closed the door behind Cubano, the Americans spotted Bailey walking toward the vehicle, flanked by two dark haired Argentine girls, and with a grin on his face.

"Check out our man over there," El Negro said in English.

"He's done alright for himself," Barbosa responded.

When the freelance writer reached the cab, Pata and Petchie exchanged a disapproving glance. They had heard Bailey was friendly with one of the players on the Old Boys team. That made him a traitor of sorts in the neighborhood of Villa Lujan. They moved aside as he approached with the girls. Bailey stopped before getting in the car and kissed them both on their cheeks.

"I'll meet you for lunch at the park tomorrow and we can work on your English some more," he said, sliding into the back seat of Gordo's taxi.

As Gordo prepared to pull away, two other girls came over to join their friends and the four young women peered into the taxi, chattering together. One of the girls stuck her head in the car and kissed El Negro on his cheek. Joel liked it. The commotion ceased when Gordo drove off, leaving the girls behind on the curb in front of Villa Lujan.

"Did you watch the game, or were you too busy?" Barbosa asked in English.

"It was great!" Craig responded enthusiastically.

"I thought there was going to be a brawl before it began," he continued. "It looked like those guys from Tafi Viejo wanted to mix it up."

"I know," Joel added. "I thought things were going to break out when Cabezan ran into their man."

"You should have heard some of the things the people in the stands were saying about you guys," Bailey said. "I learned that you hunted in Africa and killed a lion with a spear, Joel. And Cubano has fled Cuba because he doesn't want to represent the communists and wants to become a citizen of Puerto Rico to play on their Olympic team."

"What?" Barbosa asked, incredulous. "I've never mentioned Puerto Rico to anyone."

As the car rolled down the main thoroughfare from Villa Lujan, it passed a group of people walking alongside the road. There were a few small children accompanied by two older girls. As the taxi passed them, Gordo slowed down to turn out of the neighborhood.

When he did, Jesus got a better look at the group on the street. Esperanza was among them, the pretty young woman who had spoken to him after their game. She held the hand of a small boy, who hopped and jumped along with the others. They walked on without noticing Gordo's cab and its occupants and Jesus made no mention of her as they passed by.

The Americans gathered later that night for dinner at Rapido Franco's place. It was busy with fans from all around San Miguel de Tucuman. There had been games throughout the city earlier that evening and the Rimini was a popular post-event rendezvous spot. Marta and staff were energized, working at a fast pace to keep up with the food and drink orders. The kitchen was sizzling and popping.

Barbosa was already seated at a table with Bailey when Joel walked in and joined them. Che Che sat with some of his Old Boys teammates two tables away. Players from other teams were there as well, eating and drinking, and a few neighborhood families dined while some older citizenry, mostly men, dissected the night's athletic events.

Many of the patrons turned to get a look at the tall black man as he joined his friends for dinner. Marta appeared with a large bottle of beer and placed in front of El Negro. When he turned to thank her, she was already moving down the aisle, her tray of food balanced above her shoulder.

"Gracias, Marta," Joel called. He saw the back of her head bob in response.

"Joel can hold his beer," Bailey thought, taking note as El Negro poured himself half a glass, drank it down and refilled it in almost one motion.

Talk among them came to an abrupt pause when a massive man in blue army fatigues strode through the door. He was the thickest human being El Negro had ever seen. He wore a hat that was comically small for his head and big army boots. The huge man walked toward the kitchen carrying two large boxes. He was followed by Rapido Franco, carrying supplies of his own, calling out directions to his staff as he walked by. The proprietor acknowledged the Americans with a lift of his head and a smile.

"Not over there, Gordo," Rapido said, looking up at the giant man. "Take those boxes into the room next to the kitchen and leave them by the buffet table."

It was the Americans' first look at Sergeant Gordo of Mitre, a true giant. He was quite a bit taller than Joel, had much bigger shoulders than Che Che, and easily outweighed each of them by 200 lbs. Everyone at the restaurant seemed to know him. Gordo the giant was not an unusual sight even though he was 6'11" and 420 pounds.

El Negro watched the huge man put both boxes under one arm and push open one of the swinging doors to the kitchen area. He stopped before entering, exchanging a greeting with a smallish man, who had appeared from working in the back.

"Mudo," Rapido interrupted, walking up to the two. He handed him containers of produce. "Show Gordo where to put those boxes. Then take a look at the outside tables and pick up where you see the need."

The mute nodded. Sergeant Gordo of Mitre ducked down and followed his little friend into the kitchen. When the giant disappeared, the Americans looked at each other.

"Biggest man I've ever seen," Barbosa said.

"For real," Joel said, still looking at the swinging kitchen door.

"He's bigger than anyone in the NFL," Bailey added.

"Heard that," Joel said. "Do we play against him?"

"Without Sopa de Chancho," Barbosa joked. "In a few weeks, I think."

The Rimini's festive atmosphere was sustained until late in the evening. A tasty Argentine breaded meat dish called Milanesa was the order of choice among the Americans. Joel and Bailey kept Marta busy bringing quarts of beer and people from around town stopped by their table to say hello.

When the opportunity finally arose, Rapido Franco pulled up a chair next to the Americans. As always, he seemed happy, wiping his brow with a table napkin. Then he sat back and lit a cigarette.

"It has been a busy night, my friends," Rapido said. "I expected a crowd after the games were played, but with you here as an added attraction, more people came to eat than I thought."

He blew a puff of smoke upwards into the air.

"The big man you saw earlier, Gordo of Mitre, told me that everyone in Tucuman knows you are here and have come to play basketball for Villa Lujan. He said it is common knowledge that you will be eating your meals at my Rimini."

"It is good advertisement for me, no?" He asked, turning to Craig Bailey as he finished.

"We met the other day," Bailey said, extending his hand.

"I remember," Rapido said, "the journalist who came to Tucuman to find a story. Do you need to look any further, my friend? You have El Negro and Cubano right here!"

That thought had already occurred to Bailey.

Che Che walked over to say hello with a companion named Silvio, who was about the same age, shorter by a few inches and had thinning red hair. He and Bailey had met on the playground near Lake San Miguel. Silvio was formerly the editor of a fledgling newsletter called "El Capital," read by educated young progressive thinkers. But government troops entered one morning and demolished his shop. A gun was pointed into his face. He wanted justice, but found none. He had to let it go for his own safety. Basketball was his escape.

"Keep eating," Silvio said, shaking hands with everyone. "El Negro and Cubano, very good to meet you." he added. "We are playing pick-up tomorrow at

Tucuman BB before dinner. Can you join us?"

"You come too, Craig Bailey," Che Che said. "There will be other players there from around the league. No one has practice, so some of us get together to play ball and we rotate gyms when we can."

"That sounds great," Barbosa said.

"I'm down," Joel added. "Definitely want to run."

"And what about me?" Rapido Franco asked impishly.

He took another puff from his cigarette, his other hand resting on his stout belly. The only exercise he seemed to get was from his everyday hustle around the restaurant.

"The reason they named me Rapido Franco is because I'm very fast," he said, taking another puff. "I'm very fast at uncorking a bottle of wine; I am very fast at counting the money in the cash register; and I am very fast when my wife catches me with another woman!"

"Muy rapido, no?" he said with a laugh.

El Negro passed on a ride home, opting instead for the short walk from the Rimini to his apartment. The midnight air felt cooler and pleasant. He was glad to stretch his legs along the dimly lighted side streets.

As he walked by the park, he saw a small figure bobbing toward him in the darkness. El Negro tensed as he readied himself for the encounter, but then relaxed as he recognized the fiery cripple, Cabezan Monster, crutching along. He seemed to be wearing the same clothes as the day before.

"Hey, Negro, wait for me a minute, senor,"

called Cabezan Monster. He flipped to his hands and hurried toward Joel in his remarkable fashion.

"Part chimpanzee," Joel murmured to himself, intrigued.

"You are walking better tonight, senor," Cabezan Monster said, still on his hands. "You are not stumbling around like you did when you came out of Mendoza Notches last night."

"I had a few too many over there," Joel admitted, looking down to the cripple. "Got home just in time."

"Just before the morning sun," Cabezan Monster said, with a conspiratorial laugh, climbing back on his feet with his crutches. "And that was a good thing, Negro because I saw you fly tonight."

"You were at the game?" Joel asked, walking next to him now.

"I was with the other cripples, watching from outside through a gap in the masonry," he answered.

His crutches tapped against the sidewalk.

"Do you know, Negro, I have not always been a cripple," he began. "I was a farm worker as a boy but my legs got caught beneath a tractor that rolled over me while I was clearing some brush from a hillside. I was knocked unconscious and when I woke up, I had no more feeling in my legs."

El Negro was silent.

"What do you think of that, Negro?" he asked.

"How long has it been like this for you?" Joel asked, walking more slowly so the cripple could keep up.

"I am 34 years old, Negro," he answered. "I was 12 when it happened."

"That's a tough break," Joel said, stopping in

front of his building.

"I tell you, Negro," said the cripple, pulling up alongside him, "the normal people of Tucuman are cruel to us cripples. But they are afraid of me, Cabezan Monster, king of the cripples because I will fight anyone, senor."

"Did Uno Ojo ask you for money?" Cabezan Monster wanted to know. "He lost his glass eye and is trying to buy another one so he can rid himself of that black patch. Pepe has started calling him Black Beard, after the pirate. He hates being made fun of."

"Who's Pepe?" El Negro asked, moved by his little friend's plight.

"He's another cripple," Cabezan Monster said, beginning to crutch away. "You will meet him. All the cripples in town know that you are here to bring glory to Villa Lujan. I will come and watch you fly again, Negro. But now I am headed for the alley to see if I can beat Uno Ojo to the restaurant leftovers."

His legs swung in unison as he moved along the street, passing the church and bobbing into the night.

Joel's attention was drawn next to a female voice calling softly from the side entrance of his building.

"Good evening, Negro," said Malviva, moving into the light from the front door. She sashayed toward him, her high heels tapped lightly, slowly against the cement. Then she smiled.

"I've been waiting for you to come home," she said, raising her cheek for him to kiss. "I have been thinking about your bed and wondering if I could come up and see it again?"

She stood close to him and he smelled her perfume.

"I was just going put some music on and chill anyway," the tall black man said. "Come on up and hang out for a while."

"I love American music," Malviva said. "And I've brought you a little present, something for you to try."

A few blocks away, Barbosa was asleep in his apartment, still tired from his travels. Since signing with Manuel his life had been a blur and there had been no time to rest since his arrival in San Miguel de Tucuman.

He was awakened a few hours later by a soft knock at the door. Barbosa checked his clock. It was 3 a.m. He threw on a shirt and made his way down a single flight of stairs toward his front door. He heard another knock.

"One minute," he said. "I'm coming."

When he opened his apartment door, there was a woman standing in the dark, narrow hallway. She held her finger to her lips. By the light filtering out of his apartment, Barbosa could see her face. It was Esperanza. She walked toward him with her dark hair neatly brushed and pulled back.

"Jesus," she said. "I had to come see you to say that I didn't mean to walk away so swiftly . . ."

"No importa," Barbosa said. "Come in."

She entered, then he closed the door behind her. Jesus turned on a few lights as Esperanza looked around his apartment. She was dressed in long white pants with a blue blouse. Even though she wore flats, she stood almost eye to eye with Barbosa.

Esperanza was uneasy but retained her poise, offering her cheek for him to kiss. Then she drew away. Though Barbosa made no advance, she looked more nervous now.

"I shouldn't have come," she said, turning toward the door.

"I'm glad you did," Jesus said.

Chapter 12

Chino and Indignity

There were signs of a new prosperity at the old arena at Villa Lujan. Where previously there had been only one barbeque grill outside the main gate, now there were three, grilling sausages, steaks and ribs, and sending delectable smoke throughout the busy atmosphere. The Los Lobos had just won another game, boosting their record to eight wins and no defeats.

"It's gratifying, isn't it, Jefe?" Manuel asked his friend as they rose from their seats in the VIP section. "The newspapers are covering every game now and we're on top of our division!"

"Don't forget that we're also eight for eight with the Chilean," Jefe said.

"That is a very good thing," Manuel responded. "We may need money from our winnings to pay the Americans. I have heard things are a mess in Buenos Aires."

"They haven't frozen the peso yet," Jefe pointed out. "Are you worried about the economy?"

"There are whispers about war," Manuel said. "But the rumors are only gossip at this point."

"I have heard," Jefe responded. "President Galtieri wants to reclaim the Malvinas from the British."

"For patriotic reasons," Manuel scoffed. "It will be a disaster and shatter the economy. But for now, we market our investments as we see fit and continue our mission to bring a championship to Villa Lujan."

"Then we continue on as we have been doing," Jefe said. "Our goal is within reach, no?"

"Success comes with new challenges, Jefe," Manuel said reflectively. "We knew our Americans would become the focus of our competition, but Monday will be out first big test; we play Rosario at their place. You know how rabid those fans are, especially the Indians from the outskirts of the province. They will try to provoke the Americans to fight and get thrown out."

Manuel was concerned that El Negro, in particular, may find it hard to keep his temper. Cubano seemed less likely to get rattled.

"In either case," Manuel said, "we need both of them to keep their composure and stay in the game."

"Rosario lost to the Old Boys first game of the season," Jefe said, smoking as they walked through a dark concrete hallway. "Since then, they have been undefeated. They beat Tucuman BB by two at home, but the Chilean told me the refs had been paid off."

"They will be paid off for our game, as well," Manuel predicted. "Hidalgo will see to that."

"Everyone needs money," Jefe agreed. "But you risk injury if you do not blow your whistle in favor of the Bull Dogs. Remember when the Rosario fans almost killed Rapido Franco when he was a soccer official?"

Manuel let out a guffaw.

"How could I forget?" he asked. "He gave a red card to their best player before the divisional playoffs."

"And the farmers came after him with axes," Jefe said. "In the stadium bathroom, you can still see where the hatchets were coming through the door while Rapido huddled inside, fearing for his life."

"He should have known better," Manuel said matter-of-factly. "He deserved a good thrashing."

"He would have gotten more than that if Gordo the giant hadn't arrived," Jefe chuckled. "I was there. The mob was about to break into the stall when the giant grabbed the leader of the group from behind and hoisted him above the crowd. He was still holding his ax. It was comical; he looked so surprised and helpless. Then, to everyone's amazement, Gordo set him down, took his ax away and said, 'Go home.' And that was it."

"Lucky for Rapido Franco," Manuel said. "Sergeant Gordo of Mitre has a calming way about him. But remember, we play against the giant and his team after Rosario. Gordo is not fast, but El Negro will seem like a toothpick next to him."

"The team from Mitre is 4 and 2, but they were missing their best shooter when they lost to San Miguel," Jefe said. "Now he's back and the Chilean said he is shooting the ball like a military marksmen."

"I must meet this Chilean friend of yours, Jefe," Manuel said. "He seems to know more about sports in Tucuman than our own people."

"He's been in the business a long time," Jefe acknowledged.

"But Rosario can only do so much, even if the refs are paid off," Manuel said. "El Negro had 38 points tonight with five minutes to play. The Cubano had 23, and he passed the ball around like a surgeon."

"I told you he has the eyes of a midfielder," Jefe

said. "So what do I tell the Chilean? The Los Lobos are favored against Rosario but the Americans might not be able to handle getting roughed up without any protection from the refs. They haven't seen anything yet. This will be new for them."

"I grant you that, Jefe," Manuel admitted, as they walked out of the arena. "But if they can keep their heads we should be okay."

Inside the gym, Esperanza made her way around the VIP section, hoping to make eye contact with Jesus as he came out of the locker room. She had only a few minutes before she needed to rejoin her family and friends. There were little ones she needed to escort home from Villa Lujan.

Finally, Joel, Jimmy the Kid and Romano emerged from the concrete hallway, followed by Barbosa, carrying a gym bag and drinking from a big bottle of water. As he took a sip, his eyes caught sight of Esperanza standing near the VIP section. He hadn't seen her since she surprised him with a late night visit.

Jesus gave her a discreet wave, motioning for her to stay where she was. He slipped away from his teammates and made his way over to where she was waiting, greeting her with a kiss on the cheek.

"You play basketball so well, Jesus," Esperanza said, "congratulations on your win."

"Thanks," he answered. "I was hoping I'd see you again."

"I have wanted to come by to see you, but I've been busy with my studies at the university. And when I'm at home, I have to look after my younger sisters and brothers," she explained. "My Mom is a nurse at the hospital and works nights."

"So that's why you came over so late the other night," Jesus said in an understanding tone. "You needed to wait for your mother to come home before you could leave your house."

"Yes," she admitted. "I was embarrassed I woke you. But I'm free tonight if you would like to walk around town or maybe get some ice cream."

"I'd like that," Jesus said. "I'll meet you at the fountain in the park by Town Center."

A few days later, the game against Rosario had arrived. It was a hot, humid night when Joel and Jesus walked into the Bull Dog field house, thinking they had never seen such a raucous crowd. The gym was filled to capacity for the contest against undefeated Villa Lujan and its Americans. A larger-than-usual military presence was on hand as well. Soldiers in their blue army fatigues patrolled the grounds with shotguns and pistols strapped to their waists. German shepherds waited obediently beside their uniformed handlers.

Tortuga Viejo and his team gathered in a small cinderblock room for a pre-game pep talk. The barren room smelled of various stale odors and had a slop sink in one corner. Joel took a seat on its edge and Jesus stood next to him. Most of the other members of the team were seated on some metal chairs or stretched out on the stained concrete floor.

"Tonight we will be tested but we must prove we are champions," Tortuga Viejo began. "Rosario has put together five straight wins. If we fight hard, we can beat them. Keep running fast. Play defense and give the ball to Jesus or El Negro whenever they are open. And always remember, we must not let the neighborhood down."

The old coach didn't know how prescient his words would be; the game was rough from the beginning. Flaco got knocked to the ground as the players gathered for the tipoff. A dark-skinned Rosario player named Chino, known for such antics, threw a blatant elbow right in front of the referees. But there was no whistle and no foul was called.

Jesus, having missed the encounter, saw Flaco on the ground and hustled over to offer him a hand. But the skinny forward popped up to his feet, shaking off the illegal blow.

"No pasa nada," Flaco said to Jesus, gathering himself. "Chino is that way. He's a dirty player, but we can beat them, Jesus. Let's win this game."

Chino was 6'5" with a sinewy build. His eyes were deep-set and slanted, showing his Indian roots, and his long straight black hair was held back by a red headband. As he lined up to jump center, Chino stared defiantly at El Negro the way boxers do before a fight. Joel, who had been through this many times before stared calmly back.

The ball was tossed. Joel sprang upwards quickly, provoking a few exclamations from the Rosario crowd. After sending the ball to Barbosa, El Negro sprinted toward the rim for a set-up from his teammate. It didn't take long. Jesus lofted a lob toward the side of the basket and in mid-flight, Joel caught it and slammed it home before the disapproving crowd.

A whistle shrilled and a portly official came running over waving his arms, negating the basket.

"Travel violation on you, Negro," the referee said.

"I was in the air," Joel protested. "How could I have walked?"

In the crowd, Manuel and Jefe looked at each other. The call was simply wrong. But it would be the first of many during the game.

"You were right about Hidalgo getting to the officials," Jefe said. "And he's probably paid off the local militia too."

"Let's hope El Negro can keep his head," Manuel replied. "It's going to be a long game."

As the opposition focused on containing Joel, Jesus made adjustments, delivering smart passes to teammates who were open. Out on the wing, Romano hit four long shots in a row, which opened up the game for Villa Lujan.

But the 5'7" guard folded quickly under intimidation. "If you hit another shot, I'm going to find you when you're sleeping and cut your throat," Chino told Romano, bumping him on his way to the locker room during half time.

Bailey, seated with Gordo, heard the exchange and rose from his seat near the gym's corner exit.

"Play fair, Chino," the American called out. "Call the game right," he added to the officials as they passed by.

Rosario fans responded with angry words for him. A few military guards took note of his whereabouts. Manuel and Jefe saw the exchange, and then Gordo, the cabbie, pulled Bailey down next to him and said: "Tranquilo, amigo."

Romano didn't shoot the ball again for the rest of

the game. Joel, however, became more physical as the contest went on. If Chino banged him with a shoulder, Joel threw an elbow back. Finally, Jesus delivered a bounce pass to Joel, who was posting up the Indian from Rosario. The black man caught the ball and dunked it over him with two hands. Chino, in his failed effort to stop Joel, fell to the ground and the gym went quiet.

The ref ran over, blowing his whistle. It was the only sound in the building. Jesus stood next to Joel and said in English: "This ought to be interesting."

"Foul, on you Negro," the official shouted. In the stands, Bailey stood up again, his mouth open in disbelief.

"Foul on me?" Joel asked incredulously, raising his hands in protest. This was too much. He had been battling three defenders the entire game and the officials were cheating again. The crowd reacted wildly to his gesticulation. They started chanting in unison, "El Negro es sucio (dirty)" and jumping up and down in the stands. Joel lost his cool and flipped the crowd the bird.

"Technical!" the ref called out.

The crowd cheered. Jesus tried to calm Joel, who pushed him away in frustration.

"No time to lose it over that, Joel," Barbosa said, unconcerned about the shove. "Manuel warned us about getting cheated here. Stay cool, bro."

Joel walked to other end of the court, staring back at the official and then glaring at Chino. The Rosario player smirked. He made both attempts of the initial one-and-one foul and then sunk the technical. Rosario retained possession of the ball, down three points. Jesus called time. El Negro was still hot and needed a minute to collect himself.

Chino walked past the black man and taunted, "puto!"

"I'll kick his ass," Joel said to Jesus in English. He watched Chino jog down court.

As the Los Lobos players gathered on their bench, a flustered Tortuga Viejo appealed to Barbosa for instructions. Joel sat at the end of the bench, fuming as the crowd continued its dirty song about him. He looked up and spotted Bailey seated next to Gordo in the bleachers directly opposite. They made eye contact and Craig gestured downward with both hands, urging El Negro to control his temper.

Joel looked away as a group of young men approached him stealthily from behind, holding something between them. Jesus was busy talking with Tortuga Viejo and the officials stood off to the side watching the ruckus in the stands. No one was there to stop the men from advancing toward the Los Lobos bench.

"Negro, sucio!" one of the men taunted from behind Joel. As the player turned around, another lifted an iron pail and heaved its contents at him. A bucket full of urine splashed into his face and eyes. Before Joel could react, the young men from Rosario disappeared.

Manuel saw what happened and jumped to his feet. He raced down the field house steps, heading for the Los Lobos bench. Joel was in a rage. Barbosa missed the attack, but saw something was wrong and hurried over to his friend. The angry black man started walking into the crowd, looking for retaliation.

The militia moved in to intercept him.

As the military guards closed in, hands on their weapons, Manuel arrived. He tossed a towel from the bench to Joel. The officials, who didn't see the bucket of urine thrown on the black man, were confused, unwilling to blow their whistles to resume play. By now, the guards had El Negro surrounded. Manuel intervened.

"Negro, Negro, come back," Manuel said to him urgently. "Let it go. That is nothing down here. I know what it means in the States, but really, it's just a bucket of piss. They want to get you ejected from the game."

The sweating black man took a breath and scrubbed at his face with the towel. Tortuga Viejo summoned the officials to complain. They pretended to be mystified about Joel's accusations. Jesus stepped up next to his friend with a shocked expression after he learned what had happened.

"Listen to me," Manuel said to them. "There is a 200 American dollar cash bonus for each of you if we win this game. Will that help you to forget about the piss, Negro?" Joel looked at Jesus then nodded to Manuel. The military guards relaxed and moved away from the players. An official blew his whistle to resume play.

"Come on, Joel," Barbosa said, putting an arm around the black man's waist and guiding him toward the court. "Let's get a defensive stop here and put this thing away."

Bailey made eye contact with Joel.

"Play 'possum, Joel," Craig Bailey yelled out in English.

El Negro picked up on what his new friend was saying. Bailey wanted Joel to fool his opponents into thinking his mind was not in the game; his focus distracted by anger. Barbosa acknowledged without looking at either.

"Play 'possum, Joel" Jesus echoed in the same language.

El Negro then positioned himself underneath his defensive basket, seemingly still too upset to play effectively, motioning theatrically to Tortuga Viejo, who didn't know how to react. Then, when a player for Rosario began to inbound the ball, Joel sprung. He intercepted the pass and raced the length of the court. Instead of dunking the ball, he laid it up softly against the glass for an easy duce, offering nothing remotely illegal for the refs to call.

The Los Lobos had stretched it to 12 points when the final buzzer sounded. There were no handshakes after the game and military personnel escorted the visitors to their locker room. The crowd booed them as they departed. Jefe turned to Manuel and lit a cigarette.

"Nine for nine with the Chilean," he said.

"Yes," Manuel said grimly. "But that was a close one. If El Negro had been thrown out, I don't know if Jesus could have carried us through."

Bailey was with Gordo in his cab when Joel and Jesus walked over to get in. El Negro still smelled of urine. Both players looked disgusted. Nothing in their careers had prepared them for an encounter like the one they had just endured. They were relieved to be leaving Rosario.

"Wait a minute you two," Manuel called from

across the dirt parking lot. He hurried over to them and handed each two one hundred dollar bills.

"There will be more surprises for you as the season goes on," he said. "Rosario is just one stop along the way. You held it together tonight against a team of cheats, thank you. Now go home and take a bath. You both smell like piss."

Chapter 13

A Surprise Announcement

Joel was relaxing on his balcony, with the mountains visible in the distance, when Bailey stopped by the next day. He seemed to have come to terms with the attack at the Rosario game, even accepting the idea that in this country, he was not immune to that kind of humiliation. Bailey was amazed at his composure.

"I'm not in the Big Ten back in the States," Joel said. "This is how they do things here. It's crazy. It don't make it right. But I was dunking on them in their gym. It should piss them off; I just didn't expect them to throw any on me."

"It was still pretty degrading. I couldn't believe it," Bailey said sympathetically. "Who would want to play here after something like that?"

"I don't see it like that, Craig," Joel said. "I think Manuel was right. They were just mad because Jesus and I were kicking their ass. I don't hold it against them."

Bailey had seen this kind of generosity in Joel before but was still impressed. He had been around plenty of star players in college who would not have gotten over an insult like that so quickly. The black man seemed to hold no grudges, even when they were justified. In this case, he was willing to look at the situation from the opposite point of view.

"Let me ask you something," Joel demanded, before dropping the subject. "What do you think those people at Rosario would be singing if I was playing for them and dunking on Villa Lujan?"

A knock sounded from inside the apartment, bringing an end to their conversation. The two men stood up and made their way toward the front door. Craig Bailey saw Malviva up close for the first time when Joel opened it. Her face had a slight sheen and she needed a shower. She smelled of sweat and stale artificial roses. As she offered her cheek to Joel in greeting, Bailey excused himself, slipping by quickly on his way out.

"Tell Jesus I'll see him at tonight's game," Joel called, as he closed the door behind Malviva.

"She does look good in jeans," Bailey admitted to himself as he walked out of the building. "But I wish he'd leave that woman alone. She looks like trouble."

That night, the basketball game between Villa Lujan and Mitre was not much of a contest. Even though Gordo the giant was stronger than anyone on the floor, he couldn't keep up with the lissome black man from America. Barbosa simply sent the ball up court in front of Joel and then watched him race it down for easy scores. The Los Lobos ended the competition undefeated and leading the league in victories.

The only memorable moment during the game came after the giant bumped Joel on the run. El Negro flew into the iron fence with velocity, dropping to the tile floor. It took him a few seconds to gather himself, but when he did, he grew angry at the giant. On the next play, Joel caught a sideline pass from Jesus and exploded upward to the basket, dunking forcefully over the 6'11," 420 lbs. behemoth.

Rather than get offended, Sergeant Gordo caught Joel in the air on his way down from the hoop and held him on his shoulder like a small boy. At first, Joel struggled to free himself but it was no use. The giant was too strong. El Negro had to acquiesce and allow the big man to present him to the crowd as they began singing a song about him.

"Joel, maravilloso,"

"Joel, sensacional,"

"Y dale,"

"Y dale, Negro"

"Y dale que tenemos que ganar."

The giant smiled and helped Joel struggle down off his shoulder and onto the tile court.

"You ever had anything like that happen to you during a game?" Joel asked Jesus, sheepishly.

"I believe that dude could take on a grizzly bear," Jesus chuckled.

After the game, Jefe rode back to Manuel's hacienda with his friend. "I have sent Gordo to pick them up," Manuel explained, referring to his American players. "I'm going to talk to them about playing the exhibition games over dinner."

"Have you told them about President Galtieri?" asked Jefe. "If the rumors are true, shouldn't we be thinking about protecting our assets and investments?"

"I haven't mentioned it to them yet because my money is safe and I can still pay them," Manuel said. "And when we play these games up north, we'll make a small fortune. No need to say anything until then."

Back in town, a monsoon-like downpour had broken through the humidity, slapping the pavement outside the Rimini. Inside the restaurant was quiet, its doors and windows open in search of relief from the subtropical depression that had settled over San Miguel de Tucuman.

Bailey, Joel, Jesus, Pata and Petchie were gathered at a front table, drinking beers and exchanging stories, while the Americans waited for Gordo to pick them up. Their conversation was spirited and laughter erupted whenever the group was visited by Rapido Franco, who stopped by intermittently between chores.

Suddenly, a dripping stranger appeared out of nowhere and walked toward the table. His dark hair was plastered to his head and he was dirty and unshaven. Puddles of water followed his every step. He was not from town; Rapido Franco had not seen him before. Maybe he had come down from the mountains, the proprietor thought.

The stranger didn't look at anyone but Joel as he stopped at the table. The group stared back at him curiously. Up close you could see black chest hairs through his wet white shirt and that his cheeks were thin and hollow. The little man stood silently for a minute in front El Negro and the hard rain was the only sound in the restaurant until he spoke.

"I need some money, Negro," the man demanded, his accent confirming Rapido Franco's guess that the stranger was not from Tucuman. He held out his hand expectantly.

"Why are you asking me?" Joel answered quickly. "I don't know you."

"Because I know you have money, Negro, and I need some," the man said, droplets forming on his chin and falling to the floor, one after the other.

Bailey had witnessed similar encounters before, where perfect strangers approached Joel and asked him for money. Stories about his athletic prowess had spread rapidly throughout the region and most people assumed he was wealthy because of his success. Joel had shown he was sympathetic to those less fortunate than himself. But Craig noticed he gave to some and not to others and how he discriminated was as mysterious as the man now standing in front of him, holding out his hand.

Joel suddenly stood up angrily. Maybe it was the way the stranger had demanded his help. Maybe it was the way he looked at the black man. It didn't matter. He clearly had rubbed El Negro the wrong way.

"Don't be tellin' me I need to do this or that, coming up to me like you're bad!" Joel exclaimed, giving the shorter man a shove.

Rapido Franco sprang between them like an official. He ordered Marta to fetch a Rapido Special from the refrigerator. Then he asked Joel respectfully to sit back down.

"El molesta mio," El Negro said, cooperating quietly.

"He is hungry, Joel," Rapido Franco replied. "Let me handle this."

When Rapido Franco handed him a sandwich, the stranger took off the wrapper immediately, let it fall to the restaurant floor, and began eating. He turned and left as quickly as he had come without a word, worn shoes squelching on his way out.

Joel turned back to his friends. "How come

nothing like this happens to you, Jesus?" he asked, shaking his head.

"Just a drifter on the move," Rapido Franco said. "They pass through here every once in a while. He's probably looking for work in the fields."

Gordo the cab driver pulled up with his wipers flailing, barely able to keep up with the downpour. Streams of water were running beside the road now, moving swiftly past the front doors of the restaurant. The cab's tires rolled through the rivulets, making small waves as it came to a stop at the curb.

"Jesus and Joel," he called out after rolling down his window. "Vamanos! Manuel is waiting for you."

"Are you sure we should drive in this storm?" Barbosa called back through the open doors.

"Si, senor" Gordo said. "It will be fun. No one is out. The streets are empty, and Manuel has something very important to discuss with you. Vamanos, muchachos."

The big rain drops felt warm as they soaked the Americans exiting the Rimini. They hustled into Gordo's cab and drove off. Visibility was poor, but the affable cabbie was undeterred. He knew the roads, knew his car and the torrential rains bothered him little. He was jovial.

"Did you hear them singing for you tonight, Negro?" the cabbie asked. "Even Craig Bailey joined in."

Gordo began the song:

"Joel, maravilloso,"

"Joel, sensacional!"

"Yeah, I heard them," El Negro cut in. "It was wild, for sure."

"What's so important that Manuel needs to tell us?" Jesus asked. "It's pretty late for dinner."

"He didn't explain," Gordo said. "He only said it was important for me to bring you to his hacienda. Jefe is already there."

"I'll wait for you until your meeting is over," he added. "Then I will take you back home. No pasa nada."

The cab pushed on through the storm. Occasionally, it splashed waves of brownish-white water onto the windshield, blocking the road completely from view. The wipers cleared the glass for only seconds and then the driving rain would return. Street lamps became noticeably fewer as they drove out of town. Periods of darkness lasted longer as conditions worsened. The Americans looked uneasily at each other but Gordo still seemed unbothered.

"Manuel has something especially prepared for El Negro," he said, looking at the black man happily. "Jefe has brought it over from his ranchero and the chef at the hacienda has had it on the grill, cooking it on slow coals for most of the day."

"What's that?" asked Joel.

"Manuel told Jefe that you were a hunter when you were young back in Estadas Unidos," the cabbie said. "Jefe has brought some wild game for you to try. But I do not know what it is, senor. I only overheard them talking."

A streetlight in the distance grew more distinct as Gordo's cab approached. Beneath the light was a peasant woman holding a donkey on a rope. She struggled in the downpour, tugging the rope to lead the animal toward a shelter across the road. Steam rose from the sopping donkey, which was balking at the edge of the streaming road.

Gordo's headlights surprised her just as she stepped into the road ahead of the animal. The surging stream at the edge of the road was deeper than she thought. The Americans watched with dismay as the woman was swept instantly off her feet. In the dim light, they could see her turn back and reached desperately for the light post. The Renault came to a sudden stop.

The little big man threw his cab into park and flung open his door without a word, splashing toward the woman as fast as he could. Joel and Jesus looked on in amazement as Gordo waded through the rushing torrent with assurance, quickly reaching the floundering woman.

He lifted her out of the water and carried her to the middle of the road, where she was safe. He then turned back into the rushing water and moved beyond the car's headlights and out of sight. When he reappeared, the cabbie was leading the donkey through the downpour. The peasant woman bowed gratefully to her rescuer and then pulled her donkey to the other side of the road, where she disappeared from view.

"I'm telling you," Gordo said, climbing back into the cab soaking. "You can never tell what you will find in these roads on a night like this. She could have been carried into the run-off and drowned."

"You just saved her life," Jesus said with admiration.

"You are alright, Gordo!" Joel said, as he shoved

his driver's shoulder affectionately.

"For what?" the cabbie asked. "I have seen that lady and her donkey before on the side of the road. Sometimes she is pulling a cart of vegetables behind the animal. We always wave. I had to help her."

He drove off again as the Americans looked at him with new respect.

"She is luckier than the driver of the tractor that Manuel almost crashed into," Gordo said with a laugh, changing the subject. "He was in the hills up north near Salta," Gordo began, wiping at his face. "The roads are dark and windy up there. He likes to drive fast and his Peugeot is just the car for that. Around a sharp curve he came upon a tractor with no lights stopped right in front of him."

As the cabbie spoke, the Americans saw with relief they were finally approaching Manuel's hacienda.

"He hit the brakes hard," Gordo said. "His Peugeot bit the road perfectly and Manuel was able to steer his way out of it. But when he stopped, his car was facing in the opposite direction. The man driving the tractor had climbed down to see what happened. Manuel ran over and punched him in his face, knocking him down. Then he bent over and said: 'You could have killed me, you fool. Put some lights on your fucking tractor.' He hit him again and drove away."

"How do you hear these stories, Gordo?" Barbosa asked, amused.

"The boss knows that I am not a talker," Gordo said. "I do what he tells me and repeat nothing. I work for him and am invisible when it comes to business matters like Bolivia."

"Bolivia?" the basketball players repeated in confusion.

"I heard them mention the word that is all," he said, pulling in front of Manuel's. "I will wait over by the barn. There's a place I can park and dry out. When you are ready to go, send the bird dogs. They will find me right away. They always come to say hello."

Manuel greeted his guests graciously and brought them into his game room, where Jefe was working on his pool skills, smoking a cigarette. Antlered trophies mounted on the walls stared blankly across the room. Off to a corner, in front of two large windows, was a small dinner table set for four. It was midnight.

"Come take a seat, Jefe," Manuel said, walking Jesus and Joel over to their places. "It's time to eat and discuss some very interesting news with our basketball magnificos."

"Negro," Jefe called over, putting his pool stick away, "I brought some wild boar for Manuel's chef to prepare for tonight. I thought it might remind you of home, senor."

"Gracias, Jefe," Joel responded in surprise. "I shot one once when I was a boy hunting with my uncle in Alabama. We would smoke it for the whole day. Wild barbecue is the best."

A chef in a white coat appeared and filled everyone's glass with wine. He turned to a petite woman who held a tray of salads. The chef then brought out his wild boar leg, which had been draped with bacon to keep it moist while it cooked slowly over a low fire. Around the main dish were chopped pineapple, blue juniper berries and red and green grapes. An appealing aroma surrounded their table.

"And a few roasted potatoes for you, Jefe," the chef said, piling a healthy portion onto the big-bellied man's plate. The room grew quiet as the four busied themselves with dinner.

"I have some news for you," Manuel said after several minutes, his wine glass in hand. The Americans listened. "We begin a road trip this Thursday and play a game the following day in Tarija, Bolivia. I have spoken with a sportsman in the province and he is spreading the news that El Negro and Cubano from Tucuman are coming to play against a team of Bolivian all stars in Tarija. It should draw crowds from miles around."

Jefe, halfway through his plate, paused to have a smoke while he listened. Before he could light it, the petite woman appeared and struck a match for him. Joel kept eating; the food was great. Barbosa ate less heartily, but enjoyed the wild boar. Manuel finished off his wine, reached for an open bottle from an ice bucket and poured another glass.

"After the game in Tarija, we leave immediately for Salta and spend the night somewhere on the road. Then we will play Vasco de Gama from Cordoba the following evening," Manuel said. "They have two negros from America playing for them."

Joel and Jesus looked up, surprised.

"What are their names?" Joel asked, intrigued.

"One is called the Black Gaucho," Manuel said. "The other, I'm not certain. But he has played in the NBA."

The Americans glanced at one another.

"Cordoba, it's Argentina's second largest city," Manuel said. "They have a few Americans playing on teams down there."

"I have business ties in Salta and a contact at Vasco de Gama in Cordoba," Manuel continued. "We arranged a game between us on a neutral court in Salta's main arena. It will be nothing short of spectacular for fans up there. Two teams with two Americans each, all of whom bring reputations. It will be a popular ticket."

He tipped his glass and took a swallow.

"And you, my friends, will have American cash bonuses from the contests," Manuel said. He looked expectantly at El Negro and Jesus, who nodded in agreement. Jefe doused his smoke. The chef came out to fetch the remains of his wild boar leg and accept compliments on the meal. It was 2:15 a.m.

"Before I send out my Vizslas to fetch Gordo, I have one more thing I should say," Manuel began slowly. "It is none of my business whose company you choose to keep as long as you can play basketball, but I have to tell you, Joel, that Malviva is no good. Her people are no good. She will bring you trouble. It's your life, but don't let it affect what we are trying to do."

Joel was taken aback but stayed quiet. How much did Manuel know? He had been on some pretty good benders recently, and he was usually with Malviva when he partied too hard and too late.

"Jesus," Manuel said, turning to him. "I say again it is your business, but Esperanza is engaged to her childhood sweetheart who is a medical student in Buenos Aires. I feel some responsibility toward

Esperanza because her mother nursed mine before she died."

Barbosa remained expressionless.

"You would make a good card player," Manuel said to him. "I'm just asking you to be careful. But if you two keep playing as you have been I have no complaints. We are winning and making a name for ourselves. Bonuses from both games are yours if you come rested and ready to play."

Chapter 14

El Negro Crosses the Andes

As the sun came up over the Andes, an endless stretch of snow-covered peaks emerged from the darkness. A full moon glowed in the western sky, startlingly close. The terrain was desolate and barren above the tree line. "We're so high up it's like the view from a plane," Jesus thought. "Spectacular."

The bus traveled slowly as it negotiated the narrow roads and tight turns on its way to Tarija, Bolivia. It was a big touring vehicle with large windows and lots of leg room. Manuel had wanted to make sure his players could relax during the long drive. They had boarded the night before and most of the players, including Joel, had been asleep when the sun rose.

As the daylight grew stronger, the team began to wake. Tortuga Viejo was already in the front of the bus talking with the driver. Breakfast food was being passed around and the chatter among the players became louder and more animated. El Negro opened his eyes and looked out the window. He gasped.

"Stop this mother fucking bus!" Joel yelled in English, scrambling to his feet. "Where the hell are we?"

Only Jesus understood him and stood up as Joel strode down the aisle to the front. Tortuga Viejo saw him coming and didn't know what to do. The Los Lobos watched in puzzled silence. El Negro confronted the driver.

"Pare el autobus!" Joel said wildly. The driver

looked at the tall black man with confusion. He did as he was asked though, slowing his bus to a stop. Then, "Open the doors, I want to get off!" Joel ordered.

"But Negro, we have to play a game in Tarija, you can't just get off here," Tortuga Viejo pleaded.

"I'm not going any farther in this bus," he replied, his bag on one shoulder, boom box on the other. "I'm gone."

Pushing the doors open, Joel stepped down onto the road. He was surrounded by mountains and was steps away from a precipitous drop over the edge of the road. He stared at the unforgiving landscape. There were no other cars in sight.

Tortuga Viejo and Barbosa followed El Negro off the bus while the rest of the team looked on from the windows, bewildered.

"What's up, Joel?" Barbosa asked in English.

"This is scaring the shit out of me!" Joel answered. "I've never been on a road this high in my life and I'm afraid of heights. This is kickin' my ass, Jesus. I can't ride on that bus."

Tortuga Viejo listened, concerned. He didn't understand a word, but had deduced the problem. El Negro, who could jump higher than anyone he had ever seen, was now on top of the world but afraid to move. The old coach had never encountered a problem like this and didn't know how to solve it. He let Jesus do the talking.

"Joel, you've got to get back on the bus," Barbosa said to him quietly. "We're already up here and it's a long way back. Come on, bro. Just get back on and close your eyes, listen to your music."

"No way, man," he answered. "I'm not dying up

here when that bus does a nose dive off one of these mountains. I'll walk back on my own."

"What happens if night comes before you get down?" Barbosa reasoned. "You could get lost and freeze to death."

Joel shook his head but before he could answer, the Americans heard the sound of a sputtering engine and an old Ford van rounded the bend and headed toward them. There were two men in the front who waved as the dusty vehicle came to a stop behind the bus.

"Amgios, have you gotten a flat tire?" Petchie asked from the driver's window. "Why are you stopping here?"

Craig Bailey jumped down from the back of the van, where he had been riding with Goat. Pata stepped out from the passenger side and then Petchie put his vehicle into park and joined his friends.

"Man, I'm glad you guys came along," Jesus said to Craig in English. "Joel doesn't like heights. He won't get back on the bus."

"Damn right," Jefferson confirmed. "You guys want to ride over these mountains then go ahead."

"El Negro, if you don't want to ride in the bus, then why don't you come with us?" Goat asked in Spanish, surprising the American with his understanding of English.

"That's a good idea, chico," Petchie said. "I know the way and can follow the bus safely."

"You can ride up front with Petchie and Pata," Craig Bailey said. "It's closer to the ground and smaller around the turns. You'll be okay."

"I have driven this pass many times, Joel,"

Petchie assured him. "You will be safe with me."

Jefferson sighed and climbed into the dented van. As it followed the team bus through the pass, Petchie made certain to hug the safe side of the gravel road and the tall black man began to relax. Nevertheless, El Negro heaved a sigh of relief when they descended for the final time into Tarija.

It was late afternoon as they rode through town looking for Gimnasio de Llama, where they would play against the All Stars from La Paz. The game had drawn hundreds of fans to the quaint city of 200,000 residents. It was crowded with people from all regions of the Department of Tarija, which included the townships of San Lorenzo, Concepcion, Padcaya and Bermejo.

Others came from more distant cities, making their way from Santa Cruz, La Paz, Potosi, Sucre and Cochabamba. Some Argentines had even crossed over the border from Jujuy and Formosa. One businessman, interested in seeing Manuel's Americans play basketball, had traveled from Antofagasta, in northern Chile. He was considering recruiting American players for his own team.

When the Los Lobos finally stopped in front of Gimnasio de Llama, an impromptu festival was underway. Indigenous people in colorful costumes were dancing in the street and playing wooden windpipes. Pack animals were everywhere. Military soldiers, with guns at the ready, looked on impassively while bottles of singani, a potent alcoholic beverage distilled in the Bolivian Andes, were passed around freely.

"Joel, what is the first thing you notice here?"

Barbosa asked.

"Short people all around," he said.

"You got that right," Jesus said. "I feel tall among these people."

Manuel emerged from the concrete structure in front of them. His European features stood out among the shorter and darker Bolivians of Indian descent who they had passed on their way to the arena.

"Is Craig Bailey around?" Manuel asked, after he greeted the players.

"Right here," answered Bailey, who had been standing off to the side with Goat.

"Good," Manuel responded. "You travel with us tonight after the game and come to Salta. I have something brewing and may need you to play with us."

Bailey beamed. So did Goat. El Negro gave Bailey a nod. Tortuga Viejo's eyes widened. "What is brewing?" he asked himself under his breath. Barbosa strolled over to Bailey.

"Looks like we get to run together again," he said.

"The other team is warming up already and the gate is due to open any time now," Manuel said, turning back to the gym. The crowd in the street began to move in unison toward the concrete structure. They had caught sight of the Americans arriving and were gathering for a closer look.

"Let's go in before they get here," Manuel said, slipping by the military guard at the gate. His players followed. Petchie and Pata pretended to be managers, walking in with Goat behind the team.

Gimnasio de Llama was a smaller version of

Villa Lujan, with seating for 2,500. It was oblong in shape, but its playing surface was concrete instead of tile. Regulation baskets with glass backboards stood at each end of the floor. Soldiers stationed themselves around the court, keeping the crowd in order. The place filled up quickly; soon there was standing room only.

"What did I tell you, Jefe?" Manuel said. "Rumors of El Negro and Cubano have spread through the Andes like the wind. We didn't spend one peso on advertising and the gym is full."

"Do you see the referees?" Jefe asked. "Look closely at the official standing at mid court, holding the game ball. He looks identical to the Bolivian player wearing number 32."

"They are twins!" Manuel exclaimed, comparing the two men. "That doesn't bode well for Villa Lujan, does it?"

The La Paz All Stars were as motley a crew as Villa Lujan, with half the team appearing to be Amerindians, who assimilated from indigenous tribes. The other half looked more European in ancestry. Their tallest player was a lighter-skinned Latino, standing 6'4", apparently of German descent; the name printed on the back of his jersey was Kleinschmidt. The team had two guards smaller than Romano, the Los Lobos 5'7" shooting guard. The rest of the Bolivian players were somewhere in between. Their matching uniforms were the same colors as the country's flag, with horizontal bands of red, yellow and green.

In the stands, Bolivians in their bright colors bounced up and down, singing and chanting for their team. A drum sounded from somewhere. Looking around, Bailey noticed that everyone seemed to be speaking different languages. Must be local dialects, he thought. But when they cheered, they joined together in the same version of Spanish.

The crowd roared when the ball was tossed to start the game. Joel sprang up for it quickly, tipping it to Jesus. The black man proceeded to run for the rim, followed by three opposing players, including Kleinschmidt. Seeing the crowd around Joel, Barbosa launched a smooth jumper from the front of the arc. It dropped through cleanly.

Kleinschmidt quickly assumed a role as the team's main aggressor against Joel. Offensively, he was an unpolished player, but effective. On one occasion during the first half, he took an open shot from the corner, starting out with two hands on the ball, then dropping his left and heaving the ball toward the basket with his right hand, like a shot putter. Despite his technique, he could score.

At intermission the Los Lobos led 36 to the La Pas All Stars' 22 but the spread would have been wider if the referees hadn't ignored so many fouls against Joel.

"I told you the game would not be called evenly," Jefe said to Manuel. "The referees are letting the Bolivians do whatever they want to El Negro."

"There is not too much we can do about that," Manuel responded. "I just hope Joel is able to keep his head."

"The referees in Tucuman cheat but this is ridiculous," Joel said heatedly to Barbosa in English. The team had gathered in the back of the facility next to several domestic animal stalls. "If Kleinschmidt elbows me one more time he's going to get it."

"Let's just get this W and get back to Argentina without any trouble," Jesus responded, trying to calm him. "Those military guys out there look serious. Why don't you play off of Kleinschmidt. Don't get close enough to play physical with him. He won't be able to feel you that way and won't know where you are. You can just out leap him."

"I'll give it a try," Joel said, doubtfully.

"Come on out to the wing on offense and I'll give you the ball out there," Jesus instructed. "We can put Tanco and Cabezan down low and let them mix it up with this sorry lot."

Cubano and El Negro connected on their first four plays of the second half for scores. Suddenly, the Los Lobos were up by 22 and Kleinschmidt got angry. He posted up Joel on his offensive block and called for the ball. Ignoring Barbosa's advice, Joel pushed back. Kleinschmidt delivered a hard, illegal elbow to the black man's mid-section.

Joel doubled over. The blow had landed just right and knocked the wind out of him. There was no call. Kleinschmidt turned to shoot an easy four footer, but as he did, Jesus flew in and cupped the ball in the air before it could hit the backboard. The Cubano took off the other way, slipping by defenders as he dribbled down court. He caught Flaco open in the corner and the skinny forward lofted his two handed jumper, which swished through the net.

At the other end of the court, Joel was standing, recovering from the Bolivian's illegal elbow. But he was steaming. Barbosa didn't notice how shaken up

Joel had been, nor did anyone else in the gym, not even Kleinschmidt. The Bolivian posted up again. Just as an entry pass was thrown to him, Joel spun in front. As he intercepted the pass, the black man let Kleinschmidt have it with a powerful elbow of his own.

The Bolivian fell to the floor as the action of the game switched the other way. All nine players and both referees were running down court, with Jesus in the lead. El Negro floated a long pass to Cubano, who laid in the ball for an easy deuce. However, when an official saw Kleinschmidt at the opposite end of the court rolling in pain, he came running in, blowing his whistle and waving off the basket.

"Foul, on you Negro," the official said, pointing to Joel.

Tortuga Viejo stood up from the bench in protest. Manuel and Jefe watched from their seats, shaking their heads. Craig Bailey, Pata, Petchie and Goat booed from general admission seating while Jesus walked away, shaking his head in disbelief. A couple of Kleinschmidt's teammates jogged over to help him up off of the floor. Joel's cool was gone.

"How can you call that on me?" he asked hotly. "I'm down here and he's up there. You didn't see me do anything."

"I didn't see you do it, Negro, but I know you did it," the official said. "I should eject you from the game."

The crowd quieted. Soldiers became more alert.

"For what?" Joel asked. "You've been cheatin' the whole time."

"Technical foul!" the official hollered, turning

his head to the scorer's table to make certain that El Negro was assessed the violation.

Joel ran toward the official, who retreated a few steps. The Bolivians in the stands began to shout and point. Manuel was up, making his way down to the floor to prevent his player from causing any trouble. He was too late. Six military guards hurried on to the court past the official and pointed their rifles at El Negro. Joel stopped and put up his hands.

"Don't shoot," he said. "I was just going over to see if the player was okay. I didn't know that I fouled him."

Joel flashed his infectious grin and dropped his hands slowly. Then he heard the English word, "chill." It came from Jesus behind him. Kleinschmidt came back onto the basketball court and the officials looked him over and saw that he was okay. The soldiers lowered their guns.

"You alright?" Joel asked him.

"Let's go," Kleinschmidt answered.

The crowd cheered when play resumed. Joel, still hot, strolled by Jesus and asked him for the ball.

"I'm going to dunk it on everyone in here," he said.

Jesus complied and El Negro caught the ball on the wing and went hard to the hoop. He leaped from outside the lane, soaring to the basket. He brought the ball back behind his head and threw it down with such force you could hear the glass backboard crack. As he landed, a shower of glass rained down and the iron rim, with screws still attached, landed next to him.

Silence fell upon the arena. For the Bolivians, the

condor from Villa Lujan had done the unthinkable. He had shattered their glass backboard. No one had ever done such a thing before and there was no replacement for the broken basket. Then Kleinschmidt began to clap for El Negro in appreciation of his thunderous dunk. Soldiers put their guns down and joined in. Their captain grabbed hold of the rim and held it high. The crowd of Bolivians roared in unison then poured onto the court to celebrate. The game was called with the Los Lobos leading by 26 points.

Manuel made his way through the crowd of revelers, which gradually moved out into the street. Tortuga Viejo was instructing his players to gather their belongings and return to their bus. Joel was surrounded by Indians from all over the region. He was drinking from a bottle with them and they all wanted to touch him, the black man who could fly.

Jesus felt a hand slip into his while he was looking in another direction. When he turned, he saw the dark eyes of a young teenage Bolivian. She was of Indian decent, with a bright smile and beautiful teeth. She squeezed his hand and held it. The brown girl couldn't have been more than 15-years old. Her black hair was braided and held together with colorful twine. She said something to him that Jesus didn't understand and she disappeared into the crowd.

"Everyone onto the bus," Manuel instructed. "Craig Bailey, you come with us. Negro, get moving. We will spend the night across the border in La Quicaca. Everything has been arranged."

Pata, Petchie and Goat gave Craig Bailey a pat on the back.

"Pata and I have to get back to Tucuman to finish a welding job," Petchie said. "We'll see you when you get home."

"What about Goat?" Bailey asked, looking at the boy.

"He is with us," Petchie said. "Don't worry."

"Bring me something from Salta, Craig Bailey," Goat said.

The festival was moving, following the Los Lobos to their bus. Wading through the crowd, Jesus felt fingers and hands from those around him, eager to touch the magical Cubano. Across the street, El Negro, surrounded by Indians in cowboy hats, was drinking with them and in no hurry to leave.

As Joel finally walked across the street to join Jesus, a clear bottle of singani was thrust into his hand. He looked down and a cowboy, more than a foot shorter than El Negro, said something to the black man. But Joel didn't understand him.

"Gracias," he answered.

Chapter 15

The Black Gaucho in Salta

The Los Lobos crossed back over the border and spent the night in La Quiaca, a small, dusty border town, where the accommodations were modest but sufficient for a night's sleep. It was cold when the three Americans awoke after sleeping in the same room on cots. As they walked outside, Joel pointed to an empty bottle of singani left standing next to an old wooden chair.

"Caught a good one on that last night," Joel said to Barbosa and Bailey. "That Bolivian juice has some kick to it."

Tortuga Viejo stood out in front of the adobe motel, ordering everyone to follow him to a cantina across the street. It was a good place to start the day before boarding the bus for another long ride to their next game. Manuel and Jefe had driven on the night before and would meet the Los Lobos at the arena, as they had done in Tarija.

Salta's Polideportivo Floreste was a multipurpose gym with indoor seating for 6,000. It was located near 9th of July Square, the city's lively town center, named after Argentina's independence from Spain on July 9, 1816. As the bus pulled up in front of the arena, the Los Lobos were instructed to hurry in. Manuel was there with Jefe, scanning the opposing team. An imposing black figure stood out from the rest.

"There is the negro from Vasco de Gama," Manuel said. "Not as tall as El Negro, but powerfully built."

At 6'5," Norton Hillbarn had a muscular, sculpted physique. He stood underneath his basket, palming a ball nonchalantly with one hand while deflecting teammates' missed practice attempts with his other.

"I would not want to face him in the ring," Manuel said. "What a specimen!"

"He could fight for the heavyweight title right now," Jefe said. "Just from the looks of him, I would take him over the great Teofilo."

"They have another American negro, the slender one with the long arms standing to the right of the basket -- Carlos said he played last year in the NBA," Manuel pointed out. "Wallace Stuckey is his name. He speaks no Spanish, doesn't interact with his teammates. But he is a formidable player."

"He is almost as tall as El Negro," Jefe observed.

Vasco de Gama was one of the better teams in Cordoba's upper division, which was second only to Buenos Aires within the country in terms of basketball competition. The Argentines who played alongside Stuckey and Hillbarn were much better than those who played for the Villa Lujan Los Lobos. The teams would not normally have played against each other; this matchup was orchestrated by Manuel and his business partner, Carlos Fernandez, from Cordoba.

"It's your Americans against mine," Manuel had said.

"No, senor," Carlos replied. "The Americans cancel each other out. It will be my Argentines against yours."

Joel, Jesus and Craig Bailey walked down the arena steps but before stepping onto the tiled floor, they stopped for a look at Norton Hillbarn. He was hard to miss. The black American had moved out to the corner, underneath the gym's only scoreboard, shooting long jumpers with ease.

"The brother is cut," Joel said of his physique.

"I've seen that dude before!" Bailey exclaimed in surprise. "It was in Chapel Hill four years ago. He came walking down the stairs at Carmichael Auditorium to play full court pick up. There was a bunch of pros from the NBA there, an all-star cast."

Joel and Jesus looked with interest at the Black Gaucho as the rest of the Los Lobos passed by, dropping their belongings on their bench.

"David Thompson was there," Bailey recalled. "Bob McAdoo, Randy Smith and Lloyd Free were playing. Tate Armstrong and some other guys from Duke came by. And Coach Smith's players were there too – Walter Davis, Phil Ford and Mitch Kupchak. I mean the crop of basketball players was stellar, but when that dude came walking down onto the floor everyone showed him respect. I was the only one who didn't know who he was."

"I heard one pro say, 'That's Norton Hillbarn, he don't play around,'" Bailey recalled. "He's a bad hombre."

"Where's he from?" Jesus asked.

"North Carolina somewhere," Bailey said. "But I think he played for a school out in the Pacific Northwest."

Tortuga Viejo motioned for them to join warm ups. Bailey went to find a seat strategically positioned opposite both benches so he could see the action on court as well as the coaching on the sideline. Joel and Jesus took off their sweats, and began shooting and dribbling, loosening up after a long bus ride.

"Those Argentines from Cordoba look pretty good," Jesus said to Joel in English.

"Who is going to check the 6'8" guy over there?" Joel asked, looking at an Argentine player for Vasco de Gama practicing pump fakes, with spin moves and fade-aways off the glass.

"We'll have to play zone some," Barbosa said. "Romano and Cabezan out front; you, me and Jimmy the Kid down low."

"All right, then."

El Negro shot a jumper. Jesus spun with a ball in an opposite direction. Their juices were running high in anticipation of the first real competition they'd faced all season. Barbosa kept an eye on Norton Hillbarn, then, he sized up Wallace Stuckey. Both looked like legitimate NBA players. This is why I came down here, he thought.

To the surprise of Joel and Jesus, the crowd at Polideportivo Floreste favored San Miguel de Tucuman over Cordoba. Since Tucuman Province and Salta Province shared a border, the fans felt a geographical allegiance to Villa Lujan. For tonight, the Los Lobos was their home team and El Negro was their condor.

The ball was tossed up at half court to start the game. Joel rose quickly above his 6'8" Argentine opponent. As he tipped it to Jesus, Joel heard a voice from the 'hood behind him. He knew right away it belonged to the Black Gaucho.

"Nigger can raise," Hillbarn said in English. "Give him a clap."

Jesus was on the run with Stuckey chasing after him. Joel let the talk go. He sprinted down court, joining Jesus on his right wing. Jimmy the Kid appeared on the other. Vasco was asleep. Jesus dribbled behind his back, eluded a defender and zipped a one-handed cross court pass to Joel. From 20 feet away, El Negro rose and shot a beautiful left handed jumper, with picture perfect follow through. The ball's backspin made the net twine as it swished through.

"Nigger can shoot, too!" Hillbarn said, glaring at Joel as he took the ball out of bounds.

The Black Gaucho was already testy and the game had just begun. He watched his teammate Stuckey try a one-on-one move that resulted in Joel not only blocking his shot, but tipping it to Jesus. Norton sprinted back to defend against Barbosa, but the Cubano spun around and shuffled a soft pass back to Joel, who was running up from behind. El Negro spotted up, lofting another rainbow jumper from beyond the arc. It swished through again.

"Why don't you come across half court next time, nigger?" Hillbarn said in English, taunting Joel. "You scared to come inside?"

"Don't listen to him," Jesus said under his breath. "Just keep shooting your jumper, your radar looks locked in tonight. Let the Gaucho talk. The refs are on our side. If he fouls you, they'll call it."

But Norton Hillbarn had a few spectacular moves of his own, one of which had Joel leaping high into the air after a ball that was not there. After his fake, the Gaucho laid it up cleanly off the glass for a score. It was an NBA move in the highlands of Salta.

"What are you going up for, nigger?" asked Norton, tapping the ball out of bounds after it fell through the hoop. "The ball's over here."

The 6'6" Wallace Stuckey and 5'11" Jesus Barbosa chased each other up and down the court throughout much of the first half. Joel and Norton clashed repeatedly. Finally, Joel caught the ball on the wing. Norton rushed out to him, thinking El Negro would shoot his jump shot. He had already connected on nine attempts. Instead, the lithe forward drove to the hoop and flew in for a confident dunk, landing on two feet with a thump.

When he turned around, a strong hand grabbed the front of his jersey, forcing him backwards underneath the basket. El Negro raised his arms to push Hillbarn away. The crowd became confused and play stopped. Military guards began to make their way down the arena steps toward the court.

"Where did you come from, nigger?" Norton demanded. "You think you bad because you can dunk?"

"What the fuck's wrong with you, man?" Joel asked, struggling. "You crazy?"

Suddenly, Norton looked closer at Joel and recognition dawned on his face. His scowl disappeared.

"Wait a minute, are you Jumping Joel?" he asked, releasing his jersey and stepping back.

"That's what some people called me back home," El Negro said.

"No shit!" Norton said, raising his hand to slack

five with Joel. "I didn't know. I'm sorry, man. Hey, I saw your dunk up in the Carrier. Don't know if I ever saw a brother leap over two 6'10" niggers the way you did. I figured you for the NBA. What are you doing down here?"

Soldiers came onto the court, but the Black Gaucho waved them off. Confused, they retreated toward the stairs. Norton called for the refs to begin the game again. He took the ball out of bounds and threw it to Stuckey. He and Joel jogged up court together.

"I was with the Suns for preseason camp, but they let me go," Joel said. "They thought I was trouble."

"Oh yeah," Norton said, catching the ball and making a move on El Negro, shooting a clean banker in for a score. "Me too. I was with the Sonics for a few games, but it didn't work out. They wanted me to bow down to the veterans and I said 'fuck that.' I can't be kicked in the ass."

Jesus slipped by Stuckey and fed El Negro in the corner. A long jumper swished through again.

"Damn, Joel," Norton said. "How many jumpers you made, brother?"

"Don't know, but if feels like I can make every one of them tonight," Joel said smiling.

"I know that feeling," the Gaucho said. "It's good when it comes."

During the second half the pace of the game picked up, with all four Americans playing as hard as they could. Their efforts didn't go unappreciated, particularly by a group of strangers that came into the stands late, taking up a corner behind Villa Lujan's bench. They could be seen laughing and slacking hands after each electrifying play.

"How long you been down here?" Norton asked, running alongside Jesus.

"First season," he answered. "Trying to make my way to Buenos Aires and then we'll see from there."

"Did you know you already have a rep in Cordoba?" Hillbarn asked.

Barbosa caught the ball and juked away from the Gaucho. He saw Wallace Stuckey running at him, then faked him with a hesitation dribble. Stuckey went sailing by. The 6'8" Argentine player from Vasco stepped over to help with defense. Jesus countered with a bounce pass between his legs, which found El Negro as he leaped up for a lay-in with his elbows above the rim. As the ball dropped through, he parted his hands and arms like wings before descending.

"Nice move," Norton said to Jesus. "The Magical Mexican – that's what they call you. 'Cause you do shit that makes people look stupid like that brother over there."

"But he's Cuban," Joel said, jogging up alongside them. "Why they calling him Mexican?"

"I don't know," Hillbarn replied. "I've also heard some people in Cordoba talk about 'Cochise' in Tucuman. I figure they mean Jesus. But you only have one name, Joel: El Negro!"

"They're crazy with their nicknames down here," Jefferson said. "How'd you get the Black Gaucho?"

"Because I'm dangerous," Hillbarn answered with a grin.

Norton caught a pass and put a move on Joel. El

Negro stayed with him, arms outstretched defending
against the dribble. Hillbarn tossed it high to his
center. The tall Argentine caught it, spun right and
then lobbed a pass toward the basket. Joel was too
late. The Gaucho soared up and slammed it home
behind his head with two hands. The group of young
men in the corner roared in appreciation.

"We've been working on that one," Norton said
to Joel, laughing.

"See that brother, playing defense on Cochise?"
Norton asked, running up the sideline with El Negro.
He was referring to Stuckey. "He had a couple of ten-
day contracts in the NBA and hooked onto to a team
for the rest of the season last year. So the nigger
thinks he's smarter than me because he was in the
league longer."

"Maybe he's trying to prove something," Joel
replied. Jesus threw him another long pass. Before
Norton could adjust, El Negro released a long jumper.
It was smooth, spinning backwards through the air.
He didn't need to see where it went. He could feel it.
The ball swished through.

"Damn, Joel, you've got range," Norton said
before continuing. "The brother's been walking
around Cordoba with a brief case like he's a
businessman. Sometimes he wears a suit and
sunglasses. He don't speak no Spanish and he don't
want to hear nothin' from me. So I don't tell him shit,
even though he's got the exchange rate upside down."

Joel laughed.

"Do you know what I started calling him? Norton
asked, smiling. "I call him Peso, and he don't even
get pissed off."

Joel laughed again and Jesus smiled.

"He's got game, though," Jesus said. "Pretty good size for a guard in anybody's league."

"Hey, they keeping up with your paychecks?" Norton asked suddenly. "I've heard some teams have been stiffing their players – something about the political situation causing trouble."

"Yeah, we're getting paid," Joel said, but he and Jesus exchanged concerned glances.

Wallace Stuckey then landed a running one-footed jumper from 14 feet away. Craig Bailey saw the move from his seat behind Manuel and Jefe. He tapped both men on their shoulders and leaned down.

"I haven't seen anyone shoot a one-footed jumper since Bobby Dandridge played for the Bullets," Bailey said. "It's very difficult to defend. But it is also very difficult to perfect. They teach you not to do that, but I say go ahead and do it if you can, just like Stuckey."

"Who is Bobby Dandridge?" Jefe asked Manuel as they turned back around.

"I don't know," he shrugged.

Just then a casually dressed man approached them. "Manuel Fiol?" he asked in English, extending a hand. He was slightly older than Manuel and an American. Manuel stood up.

"Si senor," he said, accepting the handshake readily. "You are Coach Sullivan from the University of Iowa," he continued in English. "How good it is to finally meet you. How was the border crossing this afternoon?"

Manuel excused himself and walked Coach Sullivan up the stairs to the arena's main landing.

They talked as they ascended, and their heads nodded amicably from time to time. They disappeared from view, but then reappeared on the other side of the arena, behind the Los Lobos' bench. The young men who had come to the game late, but were actively engaged in watching the Americans play, stood up when their coach approached. Each took turns shaking hands with Manuel until their attention was diverted by Jesus intercepting the ball at half court.

Joel saw it coming. He was already on the run, filling in on Barbosa's flank. The Black Gaucho and Wallace Stuckey were too far behind to catch up. The lone Vasco de Gama defender, a guard about the same height as Jesus, backed up as the Americans advanced. But Jesus floated a high pass above the defender's head and the Condor soared after it.

Joel jumped so high that he leaped over the defender completely, catching the ball with two hands. While he was up in the air, El Negro banged the ball off the backboard and slammed it home. The crowd roared at the feat.

"Hey ref, that's illegal," Norton said in Spanish. "You can't bang the ball on the backboard. That's a technical foul."

He tried to look accusingly at Joel but couldn't hide that he was impressed by the leap.

"Nigger, you know you can't do that."

El Negro grinned.

"What's the rule on that, Jesus?" Norton asked, heading down court next to him.

"Doesn't matter, my friend," Jesus said. "The refs are on our side tonight."

"Joel's a leapin' nigger, ain't he?" Hillbarn said.

"He jumped over the brother and he was standing up straight."

"With room to spare," Jesus added.

The Americans put on a remarkable performance. Joel's last jumper tied the game at 103 in double overtime, giving him 75 points for the outing. But the Black Gaucho had his way in the end, sinking a tough turnaround jumper with Jesus and El Negro both leaping at him defensively. It was another NBA move. The ball dropped through, giving Vasco de Gama the win 105 to 103. The crowd was on its feet in appreciation. It had been a great game.

Chapter 16

Craig Bailey Joins the NBA for a Night

"That was some play your man Craig Bailey drew up," Norton Hillbarn said to Joel, taking a swig of lager from a large glass. "That white boy knows his hoop."

The Montana Cantina, a few blocks away from Salta's main gymnasium, was crowded with sports fans who had just watched the exhibition game between the Vasco-Los Lobos all stars and the University of Iowa. The Hawkeyes were on a college tour of South America, passing through Salta on their way to Buenos Aires. The impromptu competition was arranged by Manuel, who had gotten word of the university's plans.

He sent a telegram to Coach Sullivan when the team was in Caracas, Venezuela, offering to play against them with a team of all stars. Carlos agreed to allow his American players, Norton Hillbarn and Wallace Stuckey from Vasco de Gama, to play in the game along with his 6'8' Argentine center. Craig Bailey joined Joel, Jesus and Jimmy the Kid from Tucuman.

The University of Iowa team was big, with two players at 6''9" and one who was 6'11." But Joel out-jumped all of them. The Black Gaucho hit shots that only an NBA player would make. Wallace Stuckey scored with his one-footed running jumper and Jesus dazzled even the Iowa players with his passing skills. The referees made many questionable calls in favor of the Vasco-Los Lobos.

"Jesus, what the hell is going on with the refs?" Coach Sullivan asked him during play. "They aren't calling a fair game."

"Of course not," Jesus said, with a chuckle. "They'll cheat you down here, coach. They're on our side tonight."

With ten seconds left in regulation time, Iowa led by one point. It was Vasco-Los Lobos' ball. Jesus called time. Tortuga Viejo stood up from the bench, motioning like he had a plan. But when the players came to the sideline, he stepped back and let the Americans do the talking. Norton, Joel and Jesus started to discuss an inbounds play from half court, but in the midst of their conversation, Craig Bailey interrupted.

"I've got a play," he said. "Iowa will be looking to guard all four of you and double team you wherever they can. That leaves me open. But instead of shooting, I'll toss an alley-oop lob to Jesus." He turned to Barbosa, adding, "just like in high school."

"Point guard alley-oop," Norton agreed. "Good one."

"Joel, you come high to me when I throw it inbounds," Bailey said. "I'll toss it up for you. Wallace, set up on the weak side corner and hold. The way you've been shooting, they will have to guard you out there away from the basket."

Stuckey nodded.

"Norton, start on the low block and come high to the strong side elbow and set a wide screen for Jesus. Joel, you catch the inbounds, give it back to me and head over toward the wing above Wallace. Set a stationary screen. Jesus, start with Wallace, but when he sets up in the corner, you come up off of Joel's screen and then roll around tight off of Norton's screen on the elbow. The ball will be up there waiting for you."

"Craig knows what he's doing," Joel agreed, raising his glass for drink. "His play worked great. No one in the gym saw it coming. Jesus was all by himself when he laid it in at the buzzer."

"That boy needs to get into coaching or something," Norton said.

"Didn't you see what happened after the game?" Joel asked. "Some guy from an athletic club in Salta wanted to know if Craig could come and coach their team. He saw him draw up the last play. The man offered him a job on the spot, including room and board."

"No shit," Norton said. "Is he going to take it?"

"Says he wants to be a writer," Joel said, finishing his beer with a long swig. "Don't know what he's going to do."

A waitress brought two more beers for the Americans and told them they were on the house. The front door swung open and three women in tight jeans, light jackets and low cut shirts came in. They spotted the two Americans and without hesitation walked toward their table. Norton was just getting up to leave as they approached. Joel lit up, inviting the girls to have a seat. Hillbarn offered his chair.

"My bus is leaving early tomorrow," Norton said to Joel in English. "So I've got to roll. If you come to Cordoba, swing by and check out my art gallery. It's really my lady's. She's an artist."

"Alright then," Joel answered, standing up and

clasping Norton's hand. "I'm definitely going to come check it out."

"She's got me fooling around with the paint brush too, water colors and stuff," Norton said, shaking hands with Joel. "Don't let these freaks keep you out too late."

He nodded to the senoritas. The Black Gaucho caught everyone's attention as he walked through the crowded room, wearing his cowboy hat and handmade leather boots. His impressive figure disappeared through the saloon doors. Joel began introducing himself to the women at his table. He bought them drinks.

"We saw you play in Bolivia," explained one of the women, known as Ensalada de Atun (tuna salad). The nickname came from her tangy taste, she explained with a sly grin. El Negro smiled back. "We're from Jujuy. We wanted to see you play again, so the girls and I drove over."

"I'm glad you did," Joel said, raising his glass for another swig of beer.

"This is Taranga" (grapefruit), Ensalada de Atun said, pointing to her friend. "The men at home call her that because she has such a magnificent chest, don't you think, Negro?" Joel looked at her friend for a moment and mentally agreed.

"And this is Cobritta, which is short for cobra woman," Ensalada de Atun continued. Cobritta was slender, with long flowing black hair. He noted when she excused herself to go to the ladies' room, her sensuous curves swayed smoothly.

"I would like to step out with her," Joel thought.

"Negro, Cobritta has a surprise for you in the

back of the cantina," Ensalada de Atun said. "She's waiting for you."

The tall black man stood up and finished his beer. He ordered another and told the waitress to bring the women whatever they wanted. He disappeared into a dark hallway and emerged into a room with a porch door leading outside.

"I'm here, Negro," Cobritta said, waving a hand, motioning for him to come outdoors.

The night was cool. He was glad he wore his leather jacket. There was no one else around. The woman moved closer and reached into her bag. She opened her hand and displayed a small ornate box made of soft wood.

"I have some cocaine from Bolivia," she said, taking a small spoon, dipping it in the box of powder. She took a sniff in each nose. "Would you like to try some? It's pure."

"Absolutamente," El Negro answered. She held a spoon full of powder up to his nose. He readily complied. "Thank you."

"Wait here until I make my way back to the table," Cobritta said. She offered her cheek for a kiss. "That way no one will suspect anything."

But as Joel waited outside, Ensalada de Atun appeared, holding her drink in one hand. She pressed up against him, and felt warm. The fleshy woman from Jujuy opened her other hand and revealed a little silver box. She spoon fed herself and then Negro again. Joel began to feel the drug's effects. It was the best cocaine he had ever had.

The routine was repeated a third time as Ensalada de Atun exited and Taranga came out. The woman snuggled up to the tall black man and kissed him on his cheek. Then she opened a locket hanging around her neck by rawhide string. This too had cocaine in it. She snorted two spoons, gave Negro another snort and they returned to their table inside.

The drinks went down more quickly now. Joel was in his element. He thought the girls were beautiful and wild. "Come on, Negro," Ensalada de Atun said. "It's time to go dancing."

Salta la Linda (the beautiful) was true to its nickname as the sun rose the next morning. Craig Bailey was up early, walking around town. He strolled down Mitre Street, past the historic Colonial Cabildo, which formerly housed government and military authorities, the beautiful Cathedral of Salta and Victoria Theater. Circling back to the center of town, he sat at an outdoor café and nursed a cup of coffee. He thought about whether he could live and coach in this city. It certainly was pretty, with its colonial Spanish architecture and the fresh breeze blowing in from the mountains.

He reflected with satisfaction on the night before – his surprise inbounds play had worked to perfection. And the fact the he had teamed up with four NBA-caliber players, who had listened to his instruction, was simply the most gratifying basketball experience of his life.

After the alley-oop, Jesus had leaped into the air and caught the ball with two hands. No one was near him. Iowa's Coach Sullivan, who saw the play developing, was already throwing his towel down to the floor. Barbosa completed the play by laying the basketball softly against the glass for the win as time expired.

"I was hoping to find you before you left, Craig Bailey," a voice said. The American looked up and saw the director of Gimnasio de Cafayate, who had attended last night's game. Sergio Martin had witnessed Bailey's game-winning play and was impressed enough to approach him about coaching his team in Salta. "I wanted to see if you would reconsider after a night's sleep and come here to head up our team?"

Bailey stood up to shake hands with Sergio, offering him a chair. He was an older man, with the face of a retired boxer – flattened nose, facial scars and cauliflowered ears. Some of his knuckles were callused and discolored. But his smile was friendly and his handshake firm. Sergio Martin was no longer a fighter, but remained in the sport as a trainer.

"Every once in a while, I will see an athlete perform and I can tell whether he would make a good coach or not," Sergio Martin said. "You may not be as physically talented as your friends but you have the instincts of a real coach."

Jesus Barbosa watched the encounter from a block away. After a brief exchange, Sergio Martin stood up and shook hands again. He placed a card down onto the table next to Bailey's coffee cup. The former boxer clapped the American on his back and turned back into the morning crowd milling about the main square as the city started its day.

"So, are you going to stay here and coach?" Barbosa asked. "This would be a pretty nice place to live for a while."

"I thought about it," Bailey said. "But it doesn't

feel right. I still want to be a writer. I guess I want to prove something to my old man."

"You don't have to prove anything to anybody," Barbosa said.

"Yeah, well" Bailey trailed off. "Anyway right now I'm having the time of my life being a part of this, with you and Joel."

A waiter brought Jesus a bottle of water, followed by breakfast on the house for the two Americans.

"Maybe I'll write something about this instead of the Dirty War," Bailey said. "It's way more complicated than I expected, sorting out the good guys from the bad guys in this crazy country. I don't think one freelancer is going to be able to get it right."

"I never took you seriously when you said you were chasing down atrocities," Jesus said. "You came down here hoping to play ball. And last night was way cool. Admit it." Bailey nodded with a smile.

"By the way, have you seen, Joel?" Jesus added.

"He went to meet Norton somewhere last night after dinner," Craig said. "That's the last time I saw him."

"I don't know if he made it back to the hotel," Jesus offered. "I asked the concierge this morning and he hadn't seen him."

"That could be trouble," Bailey commented. "He's a big man but I've never seen anybody drink like Joel. I've had to say goodnight to him on more than a few occasions."

"After a 75-point game, he was fired up for a 75-point night," Jesus agreed. "He definitely has a wild side, seems to gravitate toward the street, even here in

Argentina."

"But he also has a big heart," Bailey remarked. "Joel is the most unusual person I have ever met. He gives the cripples around town money and makes them feel important because he spends time with them. I've seen him walking along the street with that cripple who walks on his hands, Cabezon Monster, talking to him while he's upside down, like it's no big deal."

"I know!" Jesus said. "Cabezon Monster does double time with his hands to keep up with him."

"He is nice to the locals who follow him around town, too," Jesus added. "How about the time he went to take his first shower at Villa Lujan, and Petchie and Pata set chairs up outside the stall for an up-close look at his manhood?"

"Joel told me about that," Bailey said. "Can you imagine if that happened back home and it got out to the press?"

"He laughed it off because he knows those guys consider themselves his friends," Jesus said.

As always the food was good. The air was clean. The sun was rising and the first Train to the Clouds had departed from its downtown depot for a spectacular tourist ride up 13,000 feet to the Andes.

"Did you know Joel was a math major at Michigan? Jesus continued. "He wanted to study architectural engineering, but the basketball office told him he couldn't while he played ball."

"Why not?"

"Too tough a curriculum," Jesus said. "Pissed me off when I first heard about it. But Joel didn't want to cause problems. He wanted to play in the NBA, and he was in a good place to show off his skills to get a good look."

"But then his wild side got in the way," Bailey pointed out.

"We better get to the bus station," Jesus said. "Manuel ordered a shoot-around tonight at Villa Lujan. That's more for Joel than anybody else. He's trying to keep him in check."

The sun was higher now and it was mostly clear, with only a few clouds in the sky, promising a splendid ride back to Tucuman. Bailey and Jesus made their way through the 9th of July Square, athletic bags slung over their shoulders.

They stopped at the sound of an American voice. "You white boys going my way?" It was El Negro, wearing shades and smiling from the open window of a small cab as it stopped in front of the bus station.

"It was a wild night!"

Chapter 17

"Tu Madre"

It was early evening as Gordo swung his cab around the corner like a stuntman. There was no need to hurry, he was just having fun. He sped down the street leading to Joel's apartment, explaining to Craig and Jesus that life had been boring in Tucuman since everyone left for Bolivia. He had missed the excitement of driving his American friends around town.

"I was reduced to taking Senora Sierra to Market de Tucuman," Gordo said. "She made me wait for her while she shopped. Then she held my arm like we are together. She is very lonely, my friends."

His passengers exchanged grins.

"But I told her when I dropped her off, with no tip for my trouble, not to call me anymore, senors," Gordo said firmly. "I am a busy man."

He wheeled to his right, pulling up to the curb by Joel's building with sudden precision. It was unneeded but impressive nonetheless. There was no doubt the little big man could drive.

"Now you must get to practice because we have a championship to win!" he said, with a laugh. "The Old Boys are the only other undefeated team in the league. And we play them next week."

There she was, emerging from the front door of Joel's apartment building. There was no mistaking Malviva's strut. Her black hair was still damp, freshly brushed. She crossed the street in her jeans and heels and entered into the park, headed toward a dingier side of town.

From his balcony up above, El Negro leaned out and waved to the cab, his bare chest long and rippling with muscle. His expression was animated as he held out his hand, fingers spread wide.

"Give me five, Gordo," Joel hollered down to the cab. He went back inside.

"What does he mean when he says give me five?" asked Gordo, turning to his passengers. "Does he want me to give him five pesos?"

"He means minutes," Jesus said, "knucklehead."

"Okay, I got it," said Gordo, laughing.

Joel emerged from his doorway, looking energized although he had been up the entire night before. He had slept during the bus ride from Salta that morning, still smelling of alcohol when it arrived hours later in Tucuman. He's had a little time to catch up on his sleep, but he still seemed unusually animated, Craig thought. Joel's gym clothes, which had been recently cleaned, smelled of fresh detergent. Mixed within that odor however, was another aroma.

"Smells like a woman's cheap perfume," Bailey thought.

Malviva's name wasn't mentioned on the ride to Villa Lujan. Everyone knew that if she wasn't already a hooker, she was quickly headed in that direction, Joel included. But that didn't bother him. He liked her style, her gold tooth, her shape and the fact that she was wild, the wilder, the better. She was fun to let loose with, even if he was in northern Argentina.

And Malviva lived for the moment. She was in her physical prime and had plenty of male attention. Men loved being around her, partying with her, and sometimes buying a favor from her. Joel didn't hold that against her.

"So what if she has to work some at night to keep things together?" he had said defensively to Craig Bailey. "Have you ever been poor?"

Joel was always nice to Malviva when she came by. He would let her use his shower. And he washed her hair with his long, strong hands. She really liked that. But sometimes she would steal from him. He knew she took his NCAA ring. When he mentioned that it had disappeared from his bedroom shelf, she smiled her red lips, flashed a look of desire through her dark eyes and pressed up against him. She squeezed his leg in between hers and the ring no longer mattered.

After she had showered, El Negro would brush her hair vigorously. Malviva sat down in a wooden chair in the middle of his living room, behaving like she was at a beauty salon. Joel was her 6'8" hairdresser. Sometimes she became impatient as he tried to style her hair.

"This shit don't look good, Negro," Malviva would say, with a laugh.

"You look fine to me, girl," he would answer.

That always made her smile.

Gordo made a hard right turn in traffic, driving down a side road, honking his horn as he forced a car out of his way. The other driver reacted aggressively, turning after him and racing up beside the passenger's window. Looking out, Joel saw the car inches away. Gordo recognized the other driver with a wild guffaw and popped up in his seat.

"Hold on, mis amigos!" Gordo said. "That's

Paco, the cabbie from Cajas. He thinks he can drive. He cannot keep up with Gordo from Villa Lujan, the best driver in all of San Miguel de Tucuman."

Gordo veered into a driveway and onto a sidewalk, speeding past slower traffic. Paco, seeing the maneuver, scooted across oncoming traffic and onto the sidewalk on the opposite side of the street. Pedestrians jumped out of the way as the two cabs raced down both sides of the road. When they came to an intersection simultaneously, the Renaults bounced off the curb into traffic. Both turned right and continued on.

"Are you frightened, Negro?" Gordo asked, casting a quick glance at his companion, who had grabbed the dashboard with both hands. "Don't worry, my friend. You are safe with me."

Suddenly, Gordo made a sharp left turn into the driveway of a little house set back in the middle of a quiet block. His car tilted toward the side as he turned, not quite on two wheels, but close. When the Renault's equilibrium returned, it sped forward across the back lawn of the house and onto another driveway leading out to a sleepy street.

Paco honked his horn loudly as he missed the turn. Gordo honked back. The cab driver from Cajas drove on. The race was over.

"You see, El Negro," Gordo said. "There is nothing to worry about. You do the same against Cajas tomorrow night and I will see to it personally that you have an adventurous ride home in victory."

"Don't do me any favors!" Joel responded.

The cabbie drove through another neighborhood street and came to a stop in front of Villa Lujan. It was dark now but people were still about. News of the Los Lobos' successful road trip had the neighborhood in good spirits. Villa Lujan had beaten the Bolivians.

"Nothing like a nice quiet ride to practice," Jesus said as he climbed out of the car.

"My man is in the wrong profession," Joel said, stretching his knees as he stood up. "He should be working in the movies."

"Craig Bailey," said a stranger, who emerged from the building's shadows. He had been waiting for them to arrive. The slender young man looked like a student. He was clean shaven and his hair was groomed.

"Do you know him?" Barbosa asked in English.

"Never seen him before," Bailey said.

"You been foolin' around with any women we don't know about?" Joel asked in English.

"Nope."

"Che Che told me I could find you here," the young man said in Spanish. "I was hoping I could talk to you in private for a few minutes."

"Si senor," Bailey said, waving his friends on. "Che Che is a friend of mine. How can I help you?"

The Argentine led him back toward the fence along the street. The sound of basketballs, accompanied by voices of children, echoed from inside the gym. Outside, the early evening was still, with no cars passing by.

"I've come to see if you can help us get a story into The Washington Post," the young man said, earnestly. "I am Enrique and am with the student opposition. My cousin has just escaped from being kidnapped by the military. They are looking for him now and have taken his wife and baby away."

"Who is looking for him?" Bailey asked with surprise.

"The secret police," the young man answered. "They put him in the back of a truck and were transporting him somewhere when he got away. He thought they were going to kill him. When the guard who was with him fell asleep, my cousin, with his wrists handcuffed, leaped out and tumbled down the muddy road."

Bailey reacted with sympathy but kept his manner reserved.

"No one saw him," Enrique continued. "The soft mud saved him from injury. He kept to the countryside until he could get help. He found me two nights ago. Che Che told me that you might be able to help us with a story."

Just then Goat appeared and the conversation between the two men ceased. The boy walked up to Bailey, holding his soccer ball. Then he took note of Enrique. He had seen him around town.

"Jesus has sent me to tell you that you are needed to scrimmage with the team," Goat said. "They are about to start now."

Craig nodded as Goat returned to the gym, dribbling his soccer ball with his hands. Then Bailey turned to Enrique, who looked, back hopefully.

"I'm not sure how I can help," Craig said. "I don't have the resources or experience to take on this story myself because I know the situation is complicated."

Enrique stared with disappointment at the

pavement for a few seconds. Craig felt like a coward. His earlier talk about covering this story as a freelancer seemed incredibly naïve. Now that he was in Argentina he realized how difficult and yes, how potentially dangerous, it would be to try and report on the situation as an inexperienced journalist. Then an idea came to him.

"Have you got something to write with?" He asked the Argentine.

"Si senor."

Craig wrote down the name and phone number of The Washington Post's foreign correspondent in Buenos Aires.

"Her name is Joanne," Bailey told him. "I spoke with her a few months ago. Please use my name and say I told you to call. She's busy because she's the only correspondent working in the office, covering the entire continent by herself. But she's a good one. Stay after her if you don't get her the first time you call. I'm not sure if Joanne can help, but she may have some ideas for you."

"Thank you, Craig Bailey," Enrique said, still looking dejected. "If you think you would like to come and meet my cousin while he is in hiding, send word to Che Che. He'll know where to find us."

Bailey shook his hand and turned toward the yellow haze coming from Villa Lujan's concrete gymnasium. Enrique moved away discreetly. Both men felt empty. Craig thought he would follow up with Joanne himself and mention Enrique's request.

When the shoot-around and informal scrimmage had ended, the three Americans picked up their belongings and started for the concrete steps leading out of the arena. Above to their left, behind the VIP seats, an attractive dark haired woman with a turquoise scarf tied loosely around her neck gave a slight wave when she saw them coming.

It was Esperanza again, waiting by herself. Jesus, giving his gym bag to Bailey and clapping Joel on his back, excused himself from the trio.

"Better go see what this is about," Jesus said, moving in the direction of the VIP seats. "Catch up with you later on."

Jesus had not surfaced when Joel and Craig Bailey met for dinner. They went to the Galleon for a change, a popular establishment on the other side of Town Center. They drank a few beers and each ate a "Pollo en la Casa" sandwich, which was never a disappointment.

As Joel and Craig exited the restaurant into the city's lively center, they passed by two soldiers, standing under a palm tree, watching the night life of Tucuman unfold without incident. Their rifles were slung over their shoulders and each man had a pistol strapped to his waist.

"I've never seen so many guns around," Bailey commented. "Rifles, shotguns, handguns, automatics even. You don't ever see such a heavy arms display on the street back home."

"The hell you don't," Joel replied. "Everybody where I come from is packin' heat. I've been seeing guns since I was 12. Every time I played ball in high school, the older brothers from the neighborhood would come and watch. Almost all of them had a piece of some kind."

Bailey's high school experience was a lot more

docile, he thought. Misbehaving in class or talking back to teachers were the most common offenses. No one was packing.

"It was wild," Joel explained. "Some of them, mostly drug dealers, would buy me basketball shoes and give me money to eat some good food. They would invite me to hang out. Hoop was important to them."

"I went to a card game with some of them my senior year," Joel continued. "You had to check your gun at the door. I saw about eight of them on a shelf behind the entrance. The only thing to drink was dark-colored liquor. Some people were snorting coke, but the brothers from my neighborhood wouldn't let me do anything. 'You're a ball player,' they would say. So, I just watched."

"They were playing poker," Jefferson recalled. "There was this brother who was taking everybody's money. He was bumpin' every wager, talking shit the whole time. Finally, one brother couldn't take it anymore. He had snuck his gun in and pulled it out at the card table. The place went quiet, and everyone was staring at the man and his gun."

"It was a revolver," Joel said. "Something like a 38 Police Special."

"What are you going to do with that, nigger?" the winning player demanded. "You going to kill me with that pussy motherfuckin' fun? Go ahead then and shoot. Cause your gun ain't shit. I've got a gun that shoots 45 rounds. You hear me, nigger?"

"'45 rounds!' the brother repeated."

"Wow," Craig Bailey said.

"There was silence for a long time," Joel

explained. "Then the brother said again, 'Go ahead and shoot me, nigger, or ante up and play cards.'"

"And that was it," Joel concluded. "The other brother put his gun away and started playing cards again. Everybody started drinking and snorting like nothin' happened. Saw stuff like that all the time."

As the Americans passed through Town Center, traffic passed by slowly, people were out dining and dancing or just strolling about with no apparent destination. Soldiers stationed throughout were relaxed. It was much cooler now and the moon was high overhead. Joel and Craig turned down a darkened side street, heading away from the square.

"What I don't understand is why this government is persecuting its own people," Bailey said. "They throw nuns off of planes, steal infants away from parents and kill people without a fair trial. But then you see all these people moving about freely, having a good time and it's hard to believe the Dirty War is happening."

An army truck with a green canvas cover drove by. It was full of soldiers. You could see them sitting crowded together in the back. As it passed, the soldiers recognized the tall black man and his American companion.

"El Negro, puto, sucio," a voice called out from the back of the truck. There was laughter.

"Tu madre!" Joel responded, with an attitude.

"Stop, stop," a soldier called out.

The truck came to a halt just ahead of the Americans. Soldiers started piling out. They had their rifles with them. One soldier, who was doing the talking, had his pistol in his hand. They were all young. They came running over and some aimed their guns at the Americans.

"Get down on the ground," Joel said in English. "Put your arms out wide. Don't give them no reason to shoot."

Joel and Craig Bailey lay down in the street. They were quickly surrounded. The soldier holding the pistol touched it to El Negro's head. He felt its cold steel.

"You feel the need to say something about my mother, Negro?" he asked.

"No senor," Joel replied with his face on the pavement. "I don't know your mother. I've never seen her."

"And your American friend," the man with pistol said, "does he have something against my mother?"

"No senor," Bailey said.

"Take aim," he said,

The soldiers pointed their rifles to the backs of the Americans lying in the street.

"We will finish them off and throw their bodies into the river."

"What!" Bailey exclaimed. "Don't shoot."

The soldiers held tight. The man with the pistol touched Joel's neck with his barrel.

"It's over for you, senor," he said. "Close your eyes and pray."

Then the young men let out a chorus of loud laughter. They gathered their guns and hustled back to the truck. When the last soldier had climbed in, it drove off. The soldiers were jovial and spirited as they departed. They had their fun for the evening. A voice taunted the Americans still lying in the street.

"El Negro, puto, sucio."

Joel and Craig Bailey stood up and looked each other over. Neither had been harmed. They felt stunned by the encounter but also relieved now that the moment had passed. The soldiers and their guns were gone.

"What was that you were saying about the Dirty War being invisible?" Joel asked.

"I'm glad we didn't disappear," Craig answered, shaken.

When the two men reached the park across from the train station, they parted for the evening. Craig walked on to Jesus's apartment and Joel started for home. But when he came to the park near his building, he decided he wasn't ready to call it a night.

He took the same route through the grassy field that Malviva had taken earlier in the evening. It was not well lighted. El Negro was absorbed by the dark, walking by shadowy palm trees in search of some action.

He headed straight for Mendoza Notches, a grimy-looking restaurant by day and by night, a gathering place for the city's nefarious. It was hopping. Everyone knew him when he ducked under the doorway and entered. Someone handed him a quart bottle of beer. He took a long swig. Malviva pushed through the crowd and put her arms around him. She was in party mode.

"Come with me, Negro," Malviva said, her gold tooth shining in the light.

Malviva led Joel down a flight of circular steps at the far end of the bar. At the bottom, they walked down a hallway and into a small bathroom. She kissed El Negro on the lips then opened her white purse, pulled out a small spoon and dipped it into a glass vial of cocaine. She sniffed once. Then he sniffed four times. It was smooth.

"This should catch you up, Negro," Malviva said. "Now let's go back upstairs and party."

Joel took a long swig of beer from his quart bottle. He handed it to Malviva for her to take a drink.

"Hasta que salga el sol!" he said.

She toasted him.

"Until the sun comes up, Negro."

Chapter 18

Cripples to the Rescue

Cabezan Monster came crutching across the dark park, his legs swinging from back to front. The moon was low, morning a few hours away. It was quiet. He was the only person around. As he neared a circular fountain, he could hear the soft steady sounds of splashing water. Then he saw a long, dark object in the grass just ahead. He crutched toward it with caution, thinking maybe it was a sleeping dog, a potential hazard. But on closer inspection he recognized El Negro.

Cabezan Monster switched over to his hands and moved closer to Joel. He called out to him in a whisper, but there was no response. He leaned over the black man, who was face down in the grass, motionless.

"Negro, what happened to you?" Cabezan Monster asked. The cripple sat down and put his hand to Joel's face to check his breathing. Then he felt the side of his neck for a pulse. El Negro was alive but reeked of alcohol. The cripple tried to wake him, shoving his shoulders, but Joel remained unresponsive. He saw some vomit on the grass.

"Borracha!"

Cabezan Monster stood back up on his crutches. He wondered if El Negro had poisoned himself.

"Don't you know we have a game tonight?" the cripple asked, knowing he would get no answer. "Did you go out with that whore, Malviva, last night?"

"I told you, Negro." The cripple said in

frustration, "she is not worthy of someone like you. She is sucio. No good. Why don't you listen to me?"

"Because nobody listens to me, isn't that it, Negro?" Cabezan Monster continued sadly.

The cripple crutched over to the fountain toward a faded bronze bell mounted on a stand, bearing the image of General Marco Paz. Taking one of his crutches, he swung it against the bell, striking it twice. It served as an alert among the cripples, calling them to gather at the park when one of them needed help.

Slowly, figures began to appear in the dark from different directions. Chaco, with two clubbed feet, hobbled toward the fountain. He was followed by Pepe, with his long triangular face and half a leg, crutching along on worn wooden poles and Pedro, born with only one arm and a deformed hand. Finally, Uno Ojo made his way toward the group, bobbing left and right as he walked on his big shoe, still wearing an eye patch.

They gathered around El Negro, looking with dismay at the sorry figure who was their hero. Joel had given each of them money at one time or another and was one of the few people in town who treated them as friends. When they cheered for Villa Lujan, they were cheering mainly for El Negro. They considered him one of their own.

"He looks like he's dead," Uno Ojo whispered to Cabezan Monster.

"No, he's drunk, passed out, and I can't wake him," he answered sadly.

"We have to help him," the one-eyed cripple said. "The Los Lobos play Cajas tonight. We need to get El Negro to Senora and see if she can revive him in time for the game."

"That's easy for you to say," Cabezan Monster scoffed. "Are you going to lift him yourself and carry him to her shack?"

Just then, Pepe tapped Uno Ojo on the shoulder and pointed to a figure on the far outskirts of the park, a faint image in the dark. When the figure walked under a street light, the cripples saw a short man with a bald head and recognized him. It was the mute from Rapido Franco's restaurant.

"That's Mudo," Uno Oho said urgently to Cabezan Monster. "You're the only one among us who can catch up to him. Go and tell him we need help for El Negro."

With that, Cabezan Monster flipped over onto his hands, leaving his crutches where they fell, and began running across the park, his arms moving rapidly. It was an amazing sight. He was able to intercept Mudo before he got too far away. The group of cripples around El Negro could see the mute bend over to listen to Cabezan Monster. Then Mudo began to run down the street. The small figure of Cabezan Monster collapsed on the curb, winded from his long sprint across the park.

Shortly afterward a small tractor pulling a cart arrived at the park. When it stopped near Joel, the cripples saw that it was driven by the giant, Sergeant Gordo of Mitre, with Mudo riding next to him on the fender. The two men got down and walked over to investigate the situation.

"We must get him to Senora, Gordo," Cabezan Monster said, walking back up to the crowd on his hands. "El Negro has almost drunk himself to death." He flipped over to his crutches.

"He needs help and the Los Lobos have a game tonight against Cajas," Uno Ojo added. "We have to get him well before then."

"Was it the young woman in high heels who did this to him?" the giant asked.

"Negro did it to himself," Cabezan Monster said. "I have seen him out very late on many nights."

Gordo of Mitre bent down and lifted the limp lanky form off the ground. He carried El Negro like he was a little boy and placed him gently on the cart.

Pepe, Cabezan Monster and Uno Ojo climbed in the back next to Joel and the giant and mute drove off. The rest of the cripples stood by, watching the tractor as it moved slowly down a dark, empty street. When they reached Senora's shack on the outskirts of town, the lights were on and she stood in the doorway to meet the strange group.

Senora was in her early 70s with white hair, very few teeth and wrinkled skin. She was a healer, the daughter of an indigenous Indian shaman. Though she had no certifications or degrees, she was all the cripples could afford when they needed medical attention.

Her sharp eyes took in the scene.

"El Negro has poisoned himself with alcohol, Senora," Cabezan Monster said.

"Put him over there on the couch," she instructed.

Senora disappeared and came back with a hand full of small green leaves, a jar of some yellow substance resembling honey, and a small white bone.

She placed the bone in a copper bowl and pounded it into powder. Then she stirred the ingredients together to make a gooey liquid.

"Hold him up for me, Gordo," She told the giant. "Cabezan, tilt his head back and pinch his cheeks so that his mouth opens."

Senora spoon-fed El Negro her concoction, careful not to give him too much at once. When it was all gone, she looked at her friends and dismissed them.

"Take him home and see that he sleeps on his stomach," she said. "Maybe this will help, but we'll have to wait and see."

The following morning, shortly after daybreak, Jefe received a phone call from his Chilean friend, who was the bartender at Mendoza Notches. He frowned as he heard about the enormous quantities of liquor that El Negro had consumed just a few hours before. Then he thanked his friend for the information and immediately dialed Manuel.

"The Chilean said he chugged two bottles of pisco brandy last night, if you want to call 3:30 in the morning last night," Jefe said. "Malviva pushed him out the door and told him to go home, he was so drunk. I don't know what happened to him after that, but he can't possibly be fit to play well tonight."

"I told him to stay away from that whore, she is trouble," Manuel said. "Should we wager against our own team tonight? That would be sacrilegious. I have never done that in my life."

"It is not your fault that El Negro has no self-control," Jefe said. "But if you're a smart businessman you won't bet on him tonight."

There was no answer when Craig Bailey knocked on the door of Joel's apartment much later that day. He went back downstairs to Gordo's cab. Jesus was in the back, ready to play and looking forward to the contest. Cajas was in second place behind Villa Lujan and the Old Boys and they had some good players. The game was at the Cajas home gym so no doubt the referees would be calling it their favor. Everyone wanted to beat the Americans now.

Goat came walking by, dribbling his soccer ball down the sidewalk. He spotted Bailey and came over to investigate. The American sent him up a tree next to Joel's apartment. Goat swung down onto Joel's balcony and entered his apartment. Shortly afterwards, he reappeared through the facility's front door entrance.

"He's in bed and not moving," Goat told them. "I can't wake him."

In alarm, Craig climbed the stairs quickly and found Joel standing in his doorway, bleary-eyed and disheveled. He was moving slowly and looked sick. The black man went into the bathroom and closed the door behind him. Bailey said nothing, watching in disbelief. When Joel emerged from the bathroom, Craig saw a hint of white powder near the end of his nose.

"Before a game!" he thought to himself in dismay. "Joel, grab your shoes and let's go. Jesus is in the cab waiting. We've got to get to Cajas."

Joel said nothing. He was sick from pisco. The tall black man put his basketball sneakers on and left them unlaced. Knowing they were already running late, Bailey tried to steer Joel to the stairs but El

Negro stubbornly opted for the antiquated elevator instead. It took forever to reach the first floor. They piled into the cab and the ride to Cajas was a quiet one.

Before the game began, El Negro stayed on the bench without warming up. Jesus tried to encourage him, but Joel was in no condition to play.

"I'm sick," he told Tortuga Viejo. He looked like he had no strength. "I can't play."

The Los Lobos, who had greatly improved over the season under their American tutors, rallied to play without him. Jesus faked, wove and scored in a number of ways. The timid L'Italiano , stepped up to compete for rebounds and loose balls. Cabezan set his screens and rolled to the hoop. Romano hit a few long push shots and Jimmy the Kid showed off his athleticism. The score at half without El Negro had Cajas winning, but only by six points.

The home crowd was elated. So were the military guards surrounding the basketball court. Cajas fans were cheering so loudly it was hard to hear in the gymnasium. Joel sat droopy-eyed on the bench, unable to even offer a word of encouragement to his teammates. Craig watched El Negro with a range of emotions, from disappointment and frustration to sadness. He thought Joel looked pathetic.

Bailey was still young enough that he hadn't yet seen any of his friends succumb to addiction. That would come later in his life. At that point, still in his 20s, he couldn't understand how Joel could let everyone downs so badly.

Without El Negro's intimidating presence on the floor, Cajas was emboldened to even more aggressive play. Late in the second half, after a rally by the Los Lobos brought them to within a point of their opponent, Jesus was stopped in mid-dribble by a fist to the face, which sent him to the floor. The referees pretended not to see the flagrant foul. Villa Lujan fans reacted angrily and Cajas taunted back. The military moved in. Jesus was helped up by his teammates and started over to confront the player who punched him. The officials intervened.

Craig Bailey tried to run onto the court to help his friend, but was stopped at the edge of the stands by a guard. Two others soldiers arrived and frogmarched Bailey out of the building. Finally, calm was restored. The players moved back into position to resume the game with only a minute to go, when Jimmy the Kid walked over to the bench and confronted El Negro.

"Joel, you are the best player in my country," Jimmy said in English. "You have to come out and play for us. We might lose this game without you."

"I can't," Joel answered dismissively. "I'm sick."

"But you are the best player in my country," the boy pleaded.

The Los Lobos lost by a point. El Negro was booed as he walked out of the gym behind his dejected teammates. They were angry too. Despite their best efforts they had not been able to compensate for Joel's absence on the court. Jesus had scored 43 points in a courageous but losing effort. Jimmy the Kid had his best game and L'Italiano had played like a man. Craig didn't wait for a ride back with Jesus or Joel. He walked home by himself. This was no longer any fun for him.

Late that night, Gordo dropped Jesus in front of Manuel's hacienda. The Argentine led the young man into his office, offering him a seat. On his desk was a manila envelope. Manuel fingered it for a moment and put it back down. Barbosa wasn't certain why he was summoned and was uneasy. Manuel sighed and looked up.

"We have a problem, Jesus," Manuel said. "Because of the growing unrest in the country, our President Leopold Galtieri has frozen the peso at 11,000 per dollar and the currency is in jeopardy. There is rumor that Galtieri wants to invade the Malvinas islands to win them back from the British and reinvigorate patriotism. He thinks America will be his ally but he is a fool. I'm uncertain about my investments and can no longer pay you."

"But we are supposed to play the Old Boys for the championship in a week," Jesus responded, stunned.

"I can't help that, this is beyond my control," Manuel answered sadly. "I will honor the clause in your contract about releasing your player's pass if I can't pay you," he continued, handing him the manila envelope. "You can sell it to a buyer yourself. You have worked hard and deserve the chance to find a new team."

"Is Argentina going to war?" Barbosa asked.

"It is quite possible, but for all the wrong reasons," Manuel said. "This man is unpredictable. There is no telling where this might lead."

"Are we in danger?"

"Not yet but it would be wise to go home for a while and see what happens," Manuel advised. "I have phoned a friend of mine at River Plate in Buenos Aires. He knows what I think of you as a player and a professional. When things settle down and the market place picks up again, he will contact you."

"What about Joel?"

"Another story altogether," Manuel answered. "He is a mess. I can't help him right now, and I'm not sure what I'm going to do with him. I asked him if he wanted to go home and he said no."

"Does he know that the country might go to war?"

"He doesn't care," Manuel said. "He wants to stay. He promised to reform and stay away from Malviva but I know that's not likely to happen. He has room and board for now and is content with that. I'm going to try and trade him to another team as soon as I can."

Jesus's heart sank.

"I have arranged for your flight the day after tomorrow, Jesus," Manuel said. "Or you can stay on your own dime after that and leave when it pleases you."

The two men stood up and shook hands. Barbosa was shocked at how quickly everything had come to an end. He never expected to go back to the states so soon. But he told himself he had his pass and with Manuel's recommendation, he might eventually make it to River Plate and then move closer to another shot at the NBA. He had had enough basketball in Tucuman anyway.

"You should tell your friend, Craig Bailey, that it would be a good time for him to go home as well," Manuel said. "I was thinking about hiring him as a coach. But now, I'll probably have to put my interests in sports on hold. Things are going to get worse before they get better."

It was after midnight the next day when Esperanza knocked on Jesus' apartment door. The rumors around town had reached her. The Cubano was leaving San Miguel de Tucuman. She was heartbroken.

"Come in," Barbosa said, looking somber. "I keep telling you that you shouldn't be out so late at night by yourself."

"I've come to ask you if it is true, that you are leaving?" she asked.

"Tomorrow," Jesus responded. "Manuel arranged for the flight. I'm headed home to the States for a while."

"Will you be coming back?"

"I don't know," he said, standing close to her. "I hope so."

"Will I see you again?" she asked, putting her head into his chest. She looked up. Her eyes were filling with tears.

"I'm not sure," he said.

"But I might be pregnant," she replied.

"I don't think so, we have been very careful," Jesus said softly. "But Manuel will know how to reach me if you need to. Besides, you are engaged to be married, right?"

"If you ask me to marry you, I will call it off," she said.

"I can't do that, Esperanza," Jesus said. "You are a remarkable girl, but I'm not ready to settle down."

"I know," she said. "You have to play in the

NBA."

She kissed him on his cheek and left quickly. He heard her crying quietly on her way out. Jesus sighed and looked around his apartment. Then he put on his shoes and went out toward Town Center. He turned left down Joel's street, heading for his building. As he got closer, Jesus could see lights on in Joel's apartment. He went upstairs and knocked on the door. He could hear music and women inside.

El Negro opened the door and was surprised to find Jesus standing there. Malviva and two of her friends were in the living room. A colorful array of wine bottles, empty and half full, littered the glass table in front of the women. One of them had just brought up her head from snorting a line. "Kool and the Gang" sounded from Joel's boom box. It was 2 a.m.

"Jesus, what's up, bro?" Joel asked in English. He was wide-eyed and smelling of alcohol.

"I just want you to know that I'm out of here tomorrow," Jesus answered in English. "Manuel said the country might be going to war and he can't pay us anymore."

"He told me about that," El Negro said. "He's going to try and sell us to another team that can pay us."

"Things could get real bad down here," Jesus said. "It's a good time to go back home for a while."

"Think I'll stick it out for a little longer," Joel said. "You want to come in and do a line?"

"No thanks," Jesus responded, looking regretfully at his friend, an NBA-quality forward who was probably throwing away his last shot at a decent professional career. "Maybe I'll see you before I go."

"Definitely," Joel said. When he closed the door, Jesus could hear the volume from inside pick up again. He walked out into the night.

The next morning, Craig Bailey helped him load his bags into Gordo's cab. They stood on the corner of the park across the street from Hotel Americana. Petchie, Pata and Goat drove up and parked next to them. Coming from the direction of the train station, Cabezan Monster and Uno Ojo made their way over. Everyone shook hands with Jesus.

"I'll find you back at home," Jesus said in English to Craig. "Tell Joel I'll catch up with him when things settle down."

Just after he left, a dented Toyota pickup truck drove up and pulled over a few feet away. Craig had seen the vehicle before, one night when Malviva climbed into it. This time Joel stepped out. His long strides looked slower than usual. His afro was unkempt. He wore sunglasses. Bailey was certain he had been up all night again.

"Jesus said to tell you good bye," Bailey told him in English.

"Damn, I missed him?"

He had some trouble articulating at first.

"Why don't you come home with me, Joel?" asked Bailey. "Take the train with me to Buenos Aires and then we'll fly back to D.C. from there. You can stay with me until things blow over down here."

"Thanks, Craig, but I think I'll ride it out for now," El Negro replied in Spanish. "This is the nicest place I've ever lived."

"But it's taking you down, Joel," Craig Bailey

said. "You'll never make the NBA if you stay here. Come back to the States."

"You should go home, Negro," Cabezan Monster chimed in. "This is no good for you now."

"He is right, Negro," Uno Ojo said.

The door to the pickup opened and remained that way. A sheet of hair spilled over the window of the passenger side as Malviva leaned out.

"Come on, Negro," she called, "We got to go."

The tall black man grinned at Craig Bailey then clasped his hand tightly.

"You are my friend and brother," he said. "I'll catch up with you, Craig."

He turned and got back into the truck and it drove away. Bailey's heart sank and he shook his head. He said goodbye to Pata and Petchie and clasped hands with Uno Ojo and Cabezan Monster. Taking his bag, he started for the train across the park. Goat grabbed the suitcase from him, joining him for his short walk to the station.

"Craig Bailey, you are my friend, too," Goat said. "I hope you don't forget me. But it is time for you to leave because the people from the neighborhood say the Gurkhas are coming!"

"Who are they?"

"I don't know," Goat replied. "But they are coming."

"I won't forget you little buddy," Craig said, pulling a futbol jersey from his bag that read "Gimnasio de Cafayette." He handed it to Goat. "You told me to bring you something from Salta."

He bent down and hugged the boy and handed him a bill-fold of pesos. Goat held the money in his hand and his eyes began to fill. He buried his head in his older friend's shoulder.

"Maybe the condor will fly again," Goat said, breaking slightly away.

Craig Bailey hugged him again and boarded his train.

Chapter 19

Ten Years Later

I lost his voice as static on the telephone interrupted what he was telling me. Suddenly, the line went dead, but then it was back and El Negro tried to explain what had happened in the years since I saw him.

"Man, Craig, it got real bad down here after you left," Joel said softly. "I saw Jesus, though, but then he had to go and I couldn't reach him by phone."

"You saw, Jesus?" I asked. He didn't seem to have his thoughts organized. Jesus had moved to New York six years ago. "Where is he?"

"No one was getting paid," said my friend. "Cabezan Monster came to watch me play in Buenos Aires. I was with Independente. And then they locked me up."

"Negro, why?" I asked. "Who locked you up? How long have you been in jail?"

"I'm out of money, Craig." Joel murmured. "I didn't want to ask you for none, but I want to come home. I need help."

"I've got you covered, Joel," I said. "I'll get you a plane ticket and you can pick it up at the airport. Just come to Washington."

My wife entered the room, holding our baby. She had no idea who I was talking to. She could sense the desperation in my voice. I waved her away. She moved closer to me instead.

"Craig, I've got to get out of here," he said just above a mumble.

"Okay! Do you still have your passport? Just go to the airport and hang out. I'll get everything together from here. Call me collect from there later today."

"They took my documents," he said. "I'm supposed to get them back, but I don't know when."

"Who took them?" I asked, thinking that maybe I could get the State Department to help me.

"I'm not sure," Joel said. "Did you hear that Malviva died? She was beaten to death."

There was more static.

"There some..." his voice faded.

"Hang in there, Joel and call me later," I said urgently. "OK? Joel?"

The line went dead. After several failures to fetch him back through international operators, I phoned the State Department to see what my options were to locate Joel. I called Jesus and he joined my efforts to find him. They turned up nothing. El Negro slipped away.

The End

Afterward

Argentina basketball began its emergence on the international scene during the 1980s. It gradually became a South American powerhouse. Twenty years later, Argentina became the first country to beat a United States team whose roster was made up entirely of NBA players. In 2004, the country won the gold medal for basketball at the Athens Summer Olympics. The U.S. finished with a bronze.

About the Author

Sean Kelly has been a freelance writer for The Washington Post for 30 years on topics ranging from sports and the outdoors to wildlife conservation. He has also worked as a professional stuntman and actor for 25 years, with a long list of television and film credits, including co-starring roles. While an undergraduate at the University of North Carolina at Chapel Hill during the 1970s, Sean played two years of junior varsity basketball and had a brief tryout for legendary coach, Dean Smith. He lives in Bethesda, Maryland with his wife, Cathy, and has three daughters. This, his first novel, is based on a true story.

Made in the USA
Middletown, DE
26 October 2015